# POPA SINGER

*CARAF Books*

•

Caribbean and African Literature
Translated from French

Renée Larrier and Mildred Mortimer, *Editors*

# POPA SINGER

## RENÉ DEPESTRE

**TRANSLATED AND WITH AN INTRODUCTION BY
KAIAMA L. GLOVER**

UNIVERSITY OF VIRGINIA PRESS
CHARLOTTESVILLE AND LONDON

Publication of this translation was assisted by a grant from the French
Ministry of Culture, Centre national du livre.

This translation was made possible with the generous support of the
National Endowment for the Arts.

Originally published in French as *Popa Singer*
© 2016 by Éditions Zulma

University of Virginia Press
This translation and edition © 2024 by the Rector and Visitors of the
University of Virginia
Printed in the United States of America on acid-free paper

*First published 2024*

9 8 7 6 5 4 3 2 1

LIBRARY OF CONGRESS CATALOGING-IN-PUBLICATION DATA

Names: Depestre, René, author. | Glover, Kaiama L., translator.
Title: Popa Singer / René Depestre ; translated and with an introduction by
    Kaiama L. Glover.
Other titles: Popa Singer. English
Description: Charlottesville : University of Virginia Press, 2024. | Series:
    CARAF books: Caribbean and African literature translated from
    French | Includes bibliographical references.
Identifiers: LCCN 2023043128 (print) | LCCN 2023043129 (ebook) |
    ISBN 9780813951423 (hardcover ; acid-free paper) |
    ISBN 9780813951430 (paperback) | ISBN 9780813951447 (ebook)
Subjects: LCSH: Depestre, René—Fiction. | Haiti—History—1934–1986—
    Fiction. | LCGFT: Autobiographical fiction. | Novels.
Classification: LCC PQ3949.D46 P6713 2024 (print) | LCC PQ3949.D46
    (ebook) | DDC 843/.914—dc23/eng/20231016
LC record available at https://lccn.loc.gov/2023043128
LC ebook record available at https://lccn.loc.gov/2023043129

*Cover art:* Ornate capitals, Briar Press
*Cover design:* Cecilia Sorochin

# CONTENTS

# INTRODUCTION

*Popa Singer* is a treasure of a book. Published in Paris by Éditions Zulma, the novel narrates a pivotal moment in the life of the celebrated Haitian poet, novelist, essayist, and former militant socialist René Depestre. It is a chronicle of the dangerous year Depestre spent living in Port-au-Prince in the early days of Duvalierism, a crucial albeit relatively underexamined period in Haiti's history. An autofictional tour de force, the novel relates Depestre's intimate experience of Duvalierist violence against the grim backdrop of the wider political events of 1958. In the present of the tale, the protagonist-narrator Richard "Dick" Denizan, a thinly veiled proxy for Depestre, bears horrified witness to the initial makings of Duvalier's state. Though the novel unfolds over the course of approximately a single year, it also spirals outward in both time and space to include poignant memories from Depestre/Dick's past—his childhood in Haiti and the succession of exiles that made up so much of his adult life.

Born in the southwestern coastal town of Jacmel in 1926, during the US Marine occupation of Haiti, Depestre belongs to the post–World War II generation of artists and intellectuals who came into their own in the wake of victory over European fascism. His rich and provocative body of work— which includes twelve volumes of poetry, five essay collections, three short story collections, and three novels—spans well over fifty years, making him, without question, one of the most significant voices of twentieth-century world literature. Depestre spent the great majority of his life far from home, participating in socialist and anticolonialist struggles in the most far-flung corners of the world. As he navigated the ideological and intellectual currents of Atlantic modernity, he befriended, collaborated with, and fought alongside a constellation of twentieth-century giants—Jacques Stephen Alexis and Jean-Paul Sartre; André Breton and Aimé Césaire; Pablo Neruda and Che Guevara; Jorge Amado and Ho Chi Minh, to name just a few. Ping-ponging back and forth across the Atlantic Ocean and beyond throughout the four-odd decades of the Cold War, he brought with him an unwavering political imaginary born of and anchored in his identity as a Haitian writer.

Depestre's journey began with an initial departure from Haiti in 1946, following a five-day "revolution," a presidential coup d'état, and a subsequent political takeover by a cabal of military strongmen. How Depestre found himself at the center of these events has everything to do with his role as a poet. In April of 1945, at the age of nineteen, he self-published a sensational collection of twenty poems titled *Étincelles* (Sparks), which catapulted him to celebrity across Haiti. The publication of the volume was arguably the most important cultural event of that year. Not only did it make Depestre a household name in the country, it also earned him enough money to found, alongside a cohort of like-minded student leaders, the antiestablishment, socialist-oriented publication *La Ruche* (The beehive), a self-declared "journal for literary and political combat." True to this claim, the paper, with Depestre on its masthead as editor-in-chief, was directly responsible for launching, in January 1946, a national strike that—within less than a week—brought down the corrupt, dictatorial regime of the wartime president Elie Lescot.[1]

This moment of popular revolt, known to history as "The Five Glorious Days," or "The 1946 Revolution," marked a major transformation in Haiti's twentieth-century political landscape and, importantly for Depestre, confirmed the real revolutionary possibility inherent in literature. The event also turned Depestre into a recognized threat to the military junta that took Lescot's place and thus led to his "gentle" expulsion from Haiti that November. This was the beginning of several decades of displacement and the emergence of Depestre's self-declared "banyan" identity, the dynamic state of infinite rootedness by which he understood himself to be—though constantly in exile—somehow everywhere at home.[2]

On leaving Haiti, Depestre went first to Paris, where he plugged into the intellectual circles that had emerged in the French capital after the war. During those first years of exile, he met regularly with Pan-African anticolonialists like Aimé Césaire, Léopold Sedar Senghor, and Frantz Fanon, as well as with a dynamic wider group of avant-garde writers, among whom were André Breton, Paul Éluard, Louis Aragon, Tristan Tzara, Elsa Triolet, and Michel Leiris. He became an ardent communist during this period and played an active part in the decolonization movement, as a result of which he was expelled from French territory in 1950. Depestre and his wife Edith "Dito" Sorel, whom he had met and married in Paris in 1949, then settled in Czechoslovakia for two years, where he befriended Brazilian novelist Jorge Amado and Chilean poet Pablo Neruda, and where he remained until being driven out in 1952 due to his too vocal anti-Stalinist politics. Invited to Cuba by Nicolás Guillén, Depestre attempted to settle on the island but was arrested as a communist spy and summarily deported by Fulgencio Batista's government. He and his wife then attempted a return to Europe, but were denied residency in both Italy and France. After spending a month in Vienna, Depestre made his way to Chile, where he coordinated the 1953 Continental Congress of Culture alongside Amado and Neruda before relocating briefly to Argentina. He then went on to live for over two years in Brazil, where he worked as a teacher while also participating clandestinely in the labor movement. In 1956 Depestre returned to France and participated in the First Congress of Black Writers and Artists in Paris.

Depestre published several volumes of poetry during this time: *Gerbe de sang* (Sheaf of blood) in 1946 on his way out of Haiti; *Végétations de clarté* (Vegetations of light, 1951) and *Traduit du grand large* (Dispatched from the open sea,

1952) as he bounced around Western and Eastern Europe; and *Minerai noir* (Black ore, 1956) while living in Latin America. These collections are steeped in Depestre's dramatic, firsthand experiences as a Caribbean migrant subject to the political vicissitudes of the global Cold War. They decry the fundamental evil of colonialism and (racial) capitalism, and they reveal the broad humanist impulse that animates Depestre's political and personal choices at every port. Throughout, Eros is the through line: love, lust, and desire are the motive force behind Depestre's astonishing capacity to keep moving forward in struggle, despite the repeated undoings of his political world.

This capacity for optimism ultimately brought Depestre back to Haiti in December of 1957, after more than a decade of wandering. He was hopeful that the end to the regime of Haiti's military-leader-turned-president Paul Magloire meant good things for his beleaguered country, and he had good reason to believe that positive change was afoot. After all, he had personally known the nation's newly elected head of state, François Duvalier, as a young man in Port-au-Prince: during the difficult period of Lescot's crushing dictatorship, Duvalier had been a kind and generous doctor to the capital's urban poor; he had once even cured Depestre of a particularly severe bout of malaria without ever asking for payment.

History has shown us, of course, just how unwarranted Depestre's optimism would turn out to be. As we now know all too well, "Papa Doc" was no true friend to the Haitian people, a fact that became distressingly clear to Depestre within weeks of his return. Summoned to a meeting with Duvalier at the National Palace, he quickly grasped the Ubuesque soon-to-be-President-for-Life's intention to govern Haiti as a totalitarian "Black" state. Duvalier offered to set Depestre up with a position in the foreign affairs ministry, planning to capitalize on his old friend's national and international celebrity. But Depestre refused the post, enraging Duvalier and placing his family directly in harm's way. Put under house arrest and fearing for his life, Depestre escaped from Haiti to the brand-new Cuban republic in March of 1959. It would be nearly half a century before he made his way back home again.

*Popa Singer* evokes the historical moment of Duvalier's rise to power as significant both for Depestre's political evolution and for that of the Haitian republic as a whole. The context is the Cold War, a period when several Latin American autocrats successfully exploited US fears of communist influence in the Americas in order to secure their own power, violently abusing human rights in their respective nations with the tacit sanction and often military support of the United States. Haiti was a stark instance of this phenomenon. Under the guise of ridding the country of Leftist dissidents, Duvalier ferociously suppressed any opposition to his authority. The militant anticolonialist and socialist Depestre's brief sojourn in Duvalier's Haiti was thus harrowing, to say the least.

Tragic and ludic in equal measure, and awash in specific details of Depestre's at once terrifying and farcical encounters with the regime, *Popa Singer* dives fully into the perilousness of this moment in Haiti's history. The narrative features several of the principal political actors from the period, or their comically distorted avatars. The knowing reader will easily recognize, for example, Duvalier's "intellectual" running buddy and frequent coauthor, Black nationalist ethnologist Lorimer Denis, beneath his fictional moniker, Lorimo Bolant; the novel's Clovis Barbotog presents a fairly obvious stand-in for Duvalier's former top aide and head of the Tonton Macoutes, Clément Barbot, whose ruthlessly suppressed 1963 rebellion against Duvalier Depestre includes anachronistically; and Duvalier's minister of information Georges J. Figaro has been refashioned as the idiotically peacocking Rififo Fonthus-Figaro. Other discernible characters include Duvalier's political rivals in the 1957 elections: wealthy "Mulatto" agronomist and former senator Louis Déjoie becomes Louis Delajoie; popular liberal labor organizer and exiled interim head of state Daniel Fignolé is the novel's Daniel Fignotardif; and Clément Jumelle, communist militant candidate and (following his withdrawal from the election he believed to have been rigged in Duvalier's favor) principal leader of the opposition to the president, becomes Depestre's Marc-Antoine Grandet, target of Duvalier's deranged campaign of retribution in chapter 12.

Lesser-known political and social actors also figure in the novel, their names scrambled to varying degrees. The "Kima-Rimini Affair," glossed in a footnote in chapter 5 and mentioned several additional times throughout the narrative, references Duvalier's heinous attack on Haitian journalist, activist, and cofounder of the Ligue Féminine d'Action Sociale (Feminine League for Social Action), Yvonne Hakim-Rimpel. Depestre similarly plays name games with the conspirators in the failed coup d'état of July 1958, a botched attempt by a United States–based group of exiled Haitians and American mercenaries to seize an army barracks in Port-au-Prince and overthrow Duvalier's government. Depestre devotes the whole of chapters 10 and 11 to this astonishing episode in Haiti's past, little reported on at the time and barely noted since by historians. He bestows the three Haitian conspirators—Alix "Sonson" Pasquet, Philippe "Fito" Dominique, and Henri "Riquet" Perpignan—with the pseudonyms Sonson Pasquier, Phil Dominguez, and Angelo Albi, respectively; but the Americans Robert F. Hickey, Dany Jones, Levant Kersten, Arthur Payne, and Joe D. Walker, as well as the boat they used in the insurgency, the *Molly C,* are all explicitly named. There are also several other notable figures whose names Depestre chooses not to mask in the novel: Abderrahman is the actual pen name Duvalier used in the 1950s and '60s (minus the fanciful "von Baschmakoff" of Depestre's novel) for his dogmatic nationalist political writings; General Antonio Kébreau, Duvalier's famously cruel army chief, and former president Magloire—both of whom have robust cameos—also appear without fictional aliases.

In addition to these more and less explicit allusions to historical figures from late-1950s Haiti, Depestre reprises, almost verbatim, several sections of an article he penned for *Casa de las Américas* in 1976, at the tail end of his twenty-year sojourn in Cuba.[3] "Homo Papadocus," the article turned second chapter of *Popa Singer,* conveys Depestre's bewildered effort to reconcile the compassionate local doctor of his youth with the monster Duvalier would become a decade later. "In those days," Depestre writes in the article version of "Homo Papadocus," "he was simply Doc Duvalier, without the *papa* that the mythology of bloodthirsty power would later add to his civil status. Back then, François Duvalier was a gentle doctor who fulfilled his professional duties . . . a friendly and simple man, and he enjoyed a fine reputation in the neighborhood" (84).[4] The article is, principally, a journalistic account of *noirisme,* Duvalier's notorious doctrine of fascist "Black" power. Janus face of Negritude, the 1930s anticolonialist cultural framework that emerged in the francophone world as a concerted valorization of Blackness and African culture, noirisme amounted to an ideology of Black supremacy. Depestre likens Duvalier's mutation of Negritude into the suffocating credo of noirisme to Adolf Hitler's transformation of national socialism into Nazism:

> In Duvalier's demented mind, the concept of Negritude followed the same aberrant trajectory as did socialism in Hitler's mind. In the Nazism of the latter, we find the same criminal reversal of values. Nazism and Papadocracy are techniques of absolute oppression that emerged from the two pathological poles of global capitalism, one as the weaponized mythology of a stage of development, the other as the weaponized mythology of a stage of underdevelopment.[5] (85)

Depestre articulates the logic of Duvalier's state within the geopolitical context of Germany's imperialist project in Europe and "Yankee neocolonialism" (*neocolonización yanqui,* 86) in the Americas. Both in his article and in the novel, Duvalier is shown—despite his excessive vulgarity and ludicrous pseudoscientific musings on "race"—to be a savvy politician, well aware of how to use the persistent tensions of the Cold War to buttress his despotic power.

At the same time that he situates Haiti in an explicitly global frame, however, Depestre also emphasizes the cultural idiosyncrasy of noirisme as a crucible for Duvalier's uniquely Haitian politics of racial mystification. The novel depicts Duvalier's self-serving exploitation of Vodou, in particular, as a cover for his narcissistic self-aggrandizement, arbitrary violence, and sexual sadism. Like many other Leftist writers in the Haitian literary tradition, Depestre's work reveals his profound ambivalence with regard to Haiti's popular religion—his vexation, that is, with political and community leaders who have deployed Vodou as a tool of disempowerment, seeking to compel Haiti's most marginalized to accept the oppressive political and economic injustices that determine their collective fate.[6] The Duvalier of Depestre's novel incarnates precisely such manipulation: he engages in wanton blood sacrifice, gruesome mutilation, and other depraved "Vodou-esque" rituals in his absurd, over-the-top political performances, as well as through his self-fashioning as the incarnation of Baron Samedi, the Vodou spirit of death, a cynical ploy to inspire fear and submission among his subjects.[7]

This being said, there is another side to Depestre's portrayal of Vodou in *Popa Singer,* a portrayal that emerges out of those elements of the narrative that have only tangentially to do with Duvalier. That is, as much as *Popa Singer* is a tale of political disillusionment and disappointing return, it is just as intensely a story of joyfully rewoven family ties. At the core of this "other" story is a tribute to the author/narrator's mother, the eponymous Popa Singer, aka Dianira/Déjanira Fontoriol, aka Mama Diani. A superheroine like none other, Popa is the beating heart of Depestre's tale. Through her, Depestre summons memories of his much-beloved hometown, Jacmel, its legendary anticolonial history and glorious landscape. Through her, he draws connections between Haiti's fraught past and the nation's uncertain future.

Popa is an avatar of Depestre's own mother, also named Déjanira Fontoriol, also widowed and left to raise her five young children alone with nothing to support them beyond the money she earned from sewing. Fighting valiantly to keep her family safe from the dictator's long reach, Popa is the classic famn poto-mitan of Haitian culture, a strong woman capable of holding up her family and community by sheer force of will.[8] Popa is also, however, something provocatively else. Yes, she embodies the cultural archetype of the poto-mitan woman and, relatedly, affirms the literary trope of the Singer sewing machine, best known in the context of Aimé Césaire's celebrated prose-poem *Cahier d'un retour au pays natal* (*Notebook of a Return to the Native Land*), also premised on a nostalgic return to the Caribbean homeland: *and my mother whose legs pedal, pedal, night and day, for our tireless hunger, I was even awakened at night by these tireless legs which pedal the night and the bitter bite in the soft flesh of the night of a Singer that my mother pedals, pedals for our hunger and day and night.*[9] But while Depestre's iteration of the Césairean archetype effectively connects *Popa Singer* to a broader Caribbean literary tradition, his marvel of a matriarch is not the same. She is not a mournfully evoked footnote to a hero's story, but rather the epicenter of the narrative. She is no stalwart and dutiful keeper of the hearth, but rather a feisty tornado spinning wildly through the novel.

An unparalleled force of disorderly resistance, Popa's "many forms of feminine being made for a profoundly rhizomatic identity beneath the patronymic borrowed from that Viennese magician of theater and poetry." Her "rhizomatic identity as a *lwa-métis*" exemplifies Depestre's notion of *métissage,* most thoroughly treated in his 1998 essay collection *Métier à métisser* (The work of interweaving). With this formulation, Depestre plays on the French term for a weaving loom—*métier à tisser*—and calls for a commitment to humanist *inter*weavings capable of undoing the dangerous fantasies of racial distinction that so persistently undermine political solidarity. Popa—a Black Haitian woman inexplicably granted the gift of possession by the spirit of a white German businessman who resides, under the alias of an aristocratic Austrian poet, in a sewing machine purchased from a Jacme-lian shopkeeper (!)—brings together a panoply of elements that are unique to Depestre's political and literary universe. She is as committed to the life-sustaining dimensions of Hai-tian spirituality as she is well read in the European literary tradition; her engagement with Vodou by no means requires ignorance or subjugation. And where the dictator incarnates paternalistic, phallocratic brutality, Popa is a refuge of mater-nal, romantic, and erotic tenderness.

Perhaps most importantly, Popa's delightfully rebellious spirit sets the narrative's stylistic tone. She is prone to flights of poetic whimsy, defiant outbursts, indulgent gossip, and tremendous humor. Her meandering trips down one or an-other memory lane are so many stories within stories that often veer into passionate philosophical conversations. Her Creolized turns of phrase, frequent reliance on riddles and proverbs, and flamboyant descriptions make Depestre's nar-rative—despite the tragedy of its premise—somehow deeply funny. For these are the very same elements that characterize the novel as a whole.

Formally, *Popa Singer* can be read as a *lodyans,* a uniquely Haitian mode of oral storytelling that makes use of humor to transmit an urgent lesson or to provide critical insight re-garding a political or social situation. Its purpose is to convey local knowledge and to offer moral guidance to members of a community—to teach as it entertains. Anchored in both Vodou and the Creole language, the lodyans is highly meta-phorical and reliant on proverbial wisdom. The genre has been described by Depestre's brother-in-arms Jacques Ste-phen Alexis (the novel's Jean-Alex Aldébaran) as "unfettered narrative, the confusion of time and space; it accelerates sud-denly, then backtracks, braking gently only to take off at full tilt, full speed ahead, and falling into blithe anachronism."[10] How better to characterize both Popa's and *Popa*'s style? In bringing the embodied context of orality to the space of the printed page, Depestre conjures this precise feeling of dynamic movement and thrilling instability.

The original register of the lodyans is performance and, as its name implies, it requires the presence of an audience. So it is that, from the very start, Depestre's narrator calls out to us as readers—"hey there, my friends!"—before proceeding to spin outward in pure and unbounded linguistic indulgence, clearly enchanted by his own verbal prowess. Through excess, repetition, and never-ending lists, and with words that matter as much for their sound and rhythm as for their meaning, *Popa Singer* reminds us to be listeners. It clamors to be read aloud. Loudly, even.

This fundamental orality and the resulting complexity of Depestre's swirling, Creolized French present a breathtaking challenge to the translator, more so in *Popa Singer* than in any other of his works. Far from straightforward, with its unpredictable shifts in temporality and sudden interpellations of the reader, the story often takes off in wild directions before resolving into incisive revelation or critique. It highlights the frighteningly nonsensical speechifying of the monstrous Duvalier and his sycophantic entourage, and it exalts the lyricism of everyday women and men. It is a first-person narrative interspersed with enough dialogue to make it seem as if other voices are telling their own stories, too.

In bringing this work into the Anglosphere, a work the ninety-two-year-old Depestre once told me is both his "favorite" and "his most significant," I have sought to highlight its extraordinary aesthetic innovation. I have taken care to align my practice with what I understand to be Depestre's intentions regarding transparency and opacity, hewing as closely as possible to the syntactic and semantic peculiarities of his prose. I have also followed Depestre's lead with respect to both typeface and paratext, despite the fact that his choices reveal little by way of methodology or guiding principle. There are, for instance, many Haitian-specific terms that he might have italicized or provided footnotes for, but chose not to; there are passages that take perplexing liberties with Haitian history.

My translation of this work purposefully avoids clarifying or smoothing out the elements of the writing that baffled me as a reader of French—those moments in the text that slowed me down or brought me to a full stop, even. My aim has been to preserve that feeling of disorientation and, at times, frustration in the English reader's encounter with the novel. Rife with idiosyncratic cultural phenomena, misleading historical references, satirical appellations, double-entendres, and inside jokes, Depestre's narrative is a puzzle—in his words, "a composite of the Haitian imaginary code: human beings, animals, objects, vegetation; as well as natural phenomena (rivers, seas, cyclones, volcanoes, earthquakes); and supernatural phenomena (*lwas,* states of possession, epiphanies of Vodou gods)." The effort required to put it together—to "form a cosmic whole out of the adventure of common human being," as the novel's final words declare—is very much the point. The instability of the reading experience mimetically reproduces the atmospheric conditions of the Denizan clan's existence. These conditions are the very *Haitianasseries* that the Anglophone reader must embrace in settling into the "adoptive land" of Depestre's novel.

*Popa Singer* ends with Dick poised to flee the country for Cuba, having accepted the futility of attempting to slay the Duvalierian beast on his own. He has both his mother's and von Hofmannsthal's blessing and is cautiously optimistic about the future. It is worth noting, however, that Depestre wrote *Popa Singer* in 2001, at a far distance from the socialist militancy of his youth and middle age. Like Dick, Depestre left Haiti in March 1959 and migrated to Cuba. He then spent the next decade serving Castro's newly formed state in multiple capacities: as foreign relations minister, as a broadcaster on Radio Havana, as a member of the National Cultural Council, and as a professor at the state university in Havana. He traveled throughout the socialist world during this time—as a special diplomatic envoy to China, the Soviet Union, and Vietnam—all the while writing poetry. By 1971,

however, as the regime seemed to abandon its founding principles and was becoming alarmingly intolerant of dissent,
Depestre once again found himself persona non grata in an
inhospitable authoritarian state.

Disenchanted with the Cuban revolution and with global
communism more broadly, Depestre left Cuba for Paris in
1978 to assume a role in the United Nations. He published
*Le mât de Cocagne* (*The Festival of the Greasy Pole*) in 1979
and won the Prix Goncourt de la nouvelle for his 1982 short
story collection *Alleluia pour une femme-jardin* (Alleluia for
a garden-woman). In 1986 he resigned his UNESCO post
to dedicate himself exclusively to literature, setting up his
writing table for what would be the last time in Lézignan-
Corbières, a small village in southern France. Shortly there-
after he won the Prix Renaudot for his 1988 novel *Hadriana
dans tous mes rêves* (*Hadriana in All My Dreams*). During
his final years in Cuba and in the period immediately following, Depestre also published essay collections, among
which *Pour la révolution, pour la poésie* (For the revolution,
for poetry) in 1974 and, in 1980, *Bonjour et adieu à la
négritude* (Hello and good-bye to Negritude). Many of the
key ideas put forward in these post-Cuba writings are present in *Popa Singer.*

By the time of *Popa Singer*'s publication, Depestre had
lived through significant moments in Haitian, New World,
and Pan-African history. He was ready to take a breath and
look back over his turbulent past. That Depestre drafted the
novel at the start of the twenty-first century—at the start
of controversial Haitian political leader Jean-Bertrand Aristide's second presidency—is significant. Aristide was a figure
Depestre viewed with great wariness—a figure who was, or
risked becoming, the kind of leader Depestre had met before.
Depestre's novel thus operates, at its origins, in something of
a double time: not only does it provide an unprecedentedly
intimate look at the workings of Duvalierist state power, but
it also obliquely sheds light on what Depestre perceived to
be an unsettling reiteration of all-too-similar sociopolitical

conditions nearly fifty years later. Given, too, that the novel was not in fact published until 2016, *Popa Singer* might be understood to operate in yet a third temporality, that of the political catastrophes that have emerged in Haiti since the devastating earthquake of January 2010. From the fifteen years of foreign intervention under MINUSTAH (Mission des Nations Unies pour la Stabilisation en Haïti/United Nations Stabilization Mission in Haiti) and MINUJUSTH (Mission des Nations Unies pour l'appui à la Justice en Haïti/United Nations Mission for Justice Support in Haiti), to the assassination of President Jovenel Moïse in 2021, to the hotly contested rule of Prime Minister Ariel Henry that has followed since, Haiti's citizens have existed in a state of near constant political crisis, to which Depestre has long borne dismayed witness.

Though focused sharply on a brief moment in Haiti's very particular past, *Popa Singer* grapples with the production of political modernity on a large scale. Depestre's novel paints the portrait of a hybrid world order born of complex interactions between the North Atlantic and the Global South. Illuminating a period in Haiti's history that has been considered primarily with respect to the battles waged among "big men"—government bodies, the military, the police, and the various male actors who make up these state entities, Depestre pointedly gives space and voice to the kinds of otherwise unknown individuals who have lived the despairing events of history with dignity, hopefulness, and humor.

A whirl of memories filtered through nostalgia and emotion, *Popa Singer* offers a sustained meditation, grounded in Popa's vernacular wisdom, on what Depestre calls the "hapax" of Haitian history—the specific consequences of global predation and intra-national political dysfunction on the daily lives of Haiti's citizens. It foregrounds the marvelous and the sensual within a frame that opens onto the whole world from a singularly Haitian perspective. And while Depestre's narrative indulges in, and entertains mightily with, its evocations of the tropical and the carnivalesque, it is also a highly sophisticated work of social criticism. Its irreverent and at times ribald prose pokes fun at ignorant extra-insular portrayals of Haiti and also critiques the workings of power and disempowerment within the nation itself. Unlike Depestre's essays and earlier works of prose fiction, however, *Popa Singer* proclaims no explicit political message. Rather, it meditates wistfully on a moment of missed opportunity in hemispheric American history, crafting a simple tale of individual resistance to the coercions of ideology, and a passionate love letter to a lost and wondrous homeland.

## Notes

1. For thorough analyses of this transformative moment, see Matthew J. Smith, *Red and Black in Haiti: Radicalism, Conflict, and Political Change, 1934–1957* (Chapel Hill: University of North Carolina Press, 2009), and Kaiama L. Glover, "'The Francophone World Was Set Ablaze': Pan-African Intellectuals, European Interlocutors and the Global Cold War," *Postcolonial Studies* 24.4 (2021): 464–83.

2. The banyan tree, whose roots grow down toward the ground from atop the branches of host trees, is Depestre's preferred metaphor for the hybrid, multicontinental, and unbound existence he has led since the 1940s, an alternative to what he perceives as the more despairing notion of exile. See the chapter titled "De la créolité à l'identité-banian" (From creolité to banyan identity) in Depestre's essay collection *Le métier à métisser* (Paris: Stock, 1998).

3. Depestre, "Homo Papadocus," *Casa de las Américas* 96 (May 1976): 84–91.

4. "En aquel tiempo . . . era sencillamente Doc Duvalier, sin el *papa* que la mitología de un poder sanguinario añadiría luego a su estado civil. Por entonces, François Duvalier era un médico sereno que cumplía con sus deberes profesionales . . . un hombre amistoso y sencillo, y gozaba de buena reputación en la barriada."

5. "El concepto de *negritud* sigue en la cabeza incoherente de Duvalier la misma trayectoria aberrante que había seguido el

socialismo en la mente de Hitler. En el nazismo de este último hay un mismo vuelco criminal de los valores. Nazismo y papadocracia son técnicas de opresión total que surgieron en los dos polos patológicos del capitalismo mundial: el primero, como mitología armada de una etapa del desarrollo; el segundo, como mitología armada de una etapa del subdesarrollo."

6. See Kaiama L. Glover, "The *Zonbi* as Episteme in Haitian Prose Fiction," *A Cambridge History of Haitian Literature* (New York: Cambridge University Press, forthcoming 2024).

7. Depestre's 1979 novel *Le mât de Cocagne,* a version of which he first published in Spanish in 1975 as *El palo ensebado,* is a poignant satire that similarly denounces Duvalier's perversion of Haiti's religious practices in service of his corrupt political aims. René Depestre, *The Festival of the Greasy Pole,* translated and with an introduction by Carrol Coates (Charlottesville: University of Virginia Press, 1990). Depestre uses the same vivid sobriquet—"The Great Electrifier" ("of loins and souls," of "cooches and pricks")—to refer to Duvalier in both *Cocagne* and *Popa Singer.*

8. See, for example, Marie-José N'Zengou-Tayo, "'Fanm Se Poto Mitan': Haitian Woman, the Pillar of Society," *Feminist Review* 59 (June 1998): 118–42; Darlene Dubuisson and Mark Schuller, "Beyond poto mitan: Challenging the 'Strong Black Woman' Archetype and Allowing Space for Tenderness," *Feminist Anthropology* 2 (2022): 60–74; and Sabine Lamour, "Between Intersectionality and Coloniality: Rereading the Figure of the *Poto-Mitan* Woman in Haiti," *Women, Gender, and Families of Color* 9.2 (Fall 2021): 136–51, for in-depth analyses of this trope—its usefulness to and its constraining effects on Haitian women.

9. Translated and edited by Clayton Eshleman and Annette Smith and with an introduction by André Breton (Middletown, CT: Wesleyan University Press, 2001) 10. Derek Walcott, in his 2016 poem "Trusted House," and Lorna Goodison, in her poem "For My Mother (May I Inherit Half Her Strength)," in *Tamarind Season* (1980), similarly evoke the long-suffering

maternal figure whose labor was crucial to keeping their respective households afloat.

10. ". . . le narré en liberté, la confusion du temps et de l'espace, c'est l'accélération subite, le retour en arrière, le freinage en douceur pour repartir droit devant soi à toute vitesse, à toute bouline, et tomber dans l'anachronisme désinvolte." Jacques Stephen Alexis, "Florilège du romanesque haïtien," *Étincelles* 8/9 (May–June 1984 [January 1959]): 13–21. Cited in Georges Anglade, "Le dernier codicille d'Alexis. Sur le parcours de Jacques Stéphen Alexis dans la théorie littéraire. Du réalisme merveilleux des Haïtiens à la lodyans haïtienne. Notes pour une pratique," *Présence Africaine* 175/77 (2007–8): 555.

# BIBLIOGRAPHY

Abbott, Elizabeth. *The Duvaliers and Their Legacy*. New York: McGraw-Hill, 1988.

Alexis, Jacques Stéphen. "Du réalisme merveilleux des Haïtiens." *Présence Africaine* 8-9-10 (1956): 245–71.

Césaire, Aimé. *Cahier d'un retour au pays natal*. Paris: Présence Africaine, 2000. Translated and edited by Clayton Eshleman and Annette Smith as *Notebook of a Return to the Native Land* (Middletown, CT: Wesleyan University Press, 2001).

Couffon, Claude. *René Depestre*. Paris: Seghers, 1986.

Depestre, René. *Ainsi parle le fleuve noir*. Paris: Paroles d'Aube, 1998.

———. *Alléluia pour une femme-jardin*. Paris: Gallimard, 1981.

———. "Les aventures de la créolité, lettre à Ralph Ludwig." *Écrire la "parole de nuit": La nouvelle littéraire antillaise*. Paris: Gallimard, 1994. 159–70.

———. *Bonjour et adieu à la négritude*. Paris: Laffont, 1980, 1989.

———. *Bonsoir tendresse, autobiographie*. Paris: Odile Jacob, 2018.

———. *Cahier d'un art de vivre; journal de Cuba, 1964–1978*. Arles: Actes Sud, 2020.

———. *Comment appeler ma solitude*. Paris: Stock, 1999.

———. *Encore une mer à traverser*. Paris: La Table Ronde, 2005.

———. *Éros dans un train chinois*. Paris: Gallimard, 1990.

———. *Hadriana dans tous mes rêves*. Paris: Gallimard, 1988. Translated by Kaiama L. Glover as *Hadriana in All My Dreams* (New York: Akashic, 2017).

———. *Le mât de Cocagne*. Paris: Gallimard, 1979. Translated and with an introduction by Carrol F. Coates as *Festival of the Greasy Pole* (Charlottesville: University of Virginia Press, 1990).

———. *Le métier à métisser*. Paris: Stock, 1998.

———. *L'œillet ensorcelé et autres nouvelles*. Paris: Gallimard, 2006.

———. *Pour la révolution pour la poésie*. Montréal: Leméac, 1974.

———. *Rage de vivre: œuvres poétiques complètes*. Paris: Seghers, 2007.

———. *A Rainbow for the Christian West*. Translated and with an introduction by Colin (Joan) Dayan. Amherst: University of Massachusetts Press, 1977.

Dubuisson, Darlene, and Mark Schuller. "Beyond poto mitan: Challenging the 'Strong Black Woman' Archetype and Allowing Space for Tenderness." *Feminist Anthropology* 2 (2022): 60–74.

Glover, Kaiama L. "'The Francophone World Was Set Ablaze': Pan-African Intellectuals, European Interlocutors and the Global Cold War." *Postcolonial Studies* 24.4 (2021): 464–83.

Joqueviel-Bourjea, Marie, and Béatrice Bonhomme. *René Depestre, le soleil devant*. Paris: Hermann, 2015.

Lamour, Sabine. "Between Intersectionality and Coloniality: Rereading the Figure of the *Poto-Mitan* Woman in Haiti." *Women, Gender, and Families of Color* 9.2 (Fall 2021): 136–51.

Laroche, Maximilien. *La double scène de la représentation: Oraliture et littérature dans la Caraïbe*. Québec: Université Laval, GRELCA, 1991.

Leconte, Frantz-Antoine. *René Depestre: Du chaos haïtien à la tendresse debout*. Paris: L'Harmattan, 2016.

Munro, Martin. *Exile and Post-1946 Haitian Literature: Alexis, Depestre, Ollivier, Laferrière, Danticat*. Liverpool: Liverpool University Press, 2007.

N'Zengou-Tayo, Marie-José. "'Fanm Se Poto Mitan': Haitian Woman, the Pillar of Society." *Feminist Review* 59 (June 1998): 118–42.

Smith, Matthew J. *Red and Black in Haiti: Radicalism, Conflict, and Political Change, 1934–1957*. Chapel Hill: University of North Carolina Press, 2009.

Wylie, Hal. "Creative Exile: Dennis Brutus and René Depestre." *When the Drumbeat Changes*. Edited by Carolyn Parker and Stephen Arnold. Washington, D.C.: Three Continents Press, 1981.

# POPA SINGER

The author has written of experience which is now far and lost, but which was once part of the fabric of his life. If any reader, therefore, should say that the book is "autobiographical" the writer has no answer for him: it seems to him that all serious work in fiction is autobiographical—that, for instance, a more autobiographical work than "Gulliver's Travels" cannot easily be imagined.

—Thomas Wolfe

# PRELUDE

hey there, my friends! that big boy of hers was born feet-first and under a lucky star! ladies and gentlemen, and all others gathered here, just have a look at this, if you would: right here on this third of a Caribbean island, was it really a good idea to come into the world head wrapped in a caul and feetfirst like on one's last day on this earth? thanks be to Saint Philip and Saint James the Major, all the same—having survived the journey safe and sound, mother and son will now be able to experience the frenzied time of past and future: the offspring from this side of the Caribbean sea will ask a great deal of the compass rose of his marine animal's journey

his never-before-seen emergence from the natal melodrama of his birth will only be comparable to the lumberjack's effort that birthing him cost every muscle of the maternal womb. The Black man who planted him in there—did he have any idea that he'd set her up to carry, for a full nine months, the seed of a lifelong runaway horse? bit between his teeth, hooves to the four winds, his stallion of a son will gallop full throttle up the slopes he'll have to climb, with no leeway for screwing up those acrobatics-without-a-net that—during the Indian summer days of his writing, on the shores of the bay and of his dreams of Jacmel, in the light of homelands fashioned by the time of the plantation's white sorrows—his surges of verbal invention will be

a compass stolen from a West Indian buccaneer will serve as his guide along the branch of the sea that incubates his passions somewhere downstream of the maroons' adventures.

His partners in this maritime comedy are as likely to be the whirl of cyclones as the spiraling nights of a garden-woman, the wings of an airplane, or the wheels of a locomotive. For years at a time, wandering along some goat trail, a donkey's trot and a purebred's gallop will furnish his writerly road map with botanical recipes for creativity. The fantasies of an enchanted gardener will guide his solar eroticism through the carnival of the twentieth century's conventional wisdom. A manual for a Swiss clock, a journeyman builder's toolkit, a baptismal font in a Gothic cathedral, a treatise on Soviet witchcraft—and let's not forget the Saint Étienne Weapons and Bicycles Factory catalog—will serve as so many guardrails for his poetic state of mind.

like a nurturing mother, a big-mama spool of thread will send his enchanted kite soaring through the feminine blue skies of history, thrilled to feed its most glorious strands through the Singer sewing machine as it stitches the beautiful sheets of a Germano-Haitian marvelous real among the night terrors of those childhood years, before furnishing with French-styled rhizomes the surges of evening prose that would make the whole world hear the sonata of grief so specific to the very skin and bones of a poor devil from the Black republic

his endless tragedy will bear the names of real people: Papa Doc, Rififo Fonthus-Figaro, Clovis Barbotog, L'il Râ Bordaille, Boss Gros-Bobo, Victor-Hugo Novembre, Claudius Rémont, Francesca de Saint-Totor, Comrade Kola, Kesner Altidor, Tédéhomme Maxisextus, Chris Lafalaize, Pépé Nicolas, Jean-Alex Aldébaran, Thomas and Wilfried Monastir, Dany L'il Jones, Lucien Leprieur, Mama Simone, Maria-Carla Depester, Maria-Antonia von Brentano, Abderrahman von Baschmakoff, Jeanjean Duvalier, Lorimiro Bolant, Arthur Payne, Joe D. Walker, Robert F. Hickey, Levant Kersten, Sonson Pasquier, Angelo Albi, Phil Dominguez, Antonio Alvarez, Yvonne Kima-Rimini, Rachid Ben Estefano, Didier

Jeannotin, Pablo Picasso, Marilyn Monroe, Che Guevara, Vincent Van Gogh, and the members of the Denizan and Fontoriol families, and Lili Fontoriol hail Mary, and Carson McCullers and Dito Sorel hallelujah for the Jewish fairy of those Sorbonne days

and to the many other proper names that have darkened or illuminated his defeated poet's solitude might easily be added the list of names of the *lwa*,* Atibon Legba, Erzili Freda-Dahomey, Ogou Badagris, Damballah and Aïda Wédo, Agoué-Taroyo, Popa Singer von Hofmannsthal. Living beings and pagan gods alike have taken on their respective roles as executioners or victims in villages and hamlets bearing the names Jacmel, Port-au-Prince, Pétionville, Délugé, Trou-Foban, Cochon-Gras, Fonds-Sultane, La Croix des Bouquets, Le Bas Coq-qui-chante, Le Haut Coq-qui-chante, Anse-à-Foufoune, Bombardopolis, Saltrou for heaven's sake

Grand-Ya Fleuriblanc's eldest daughter, the very Dianira Fontoriol who is part of this escapade, aka Popa Singer von Hofmannsthal, goddaughter of General Alphénix Ultimo—by the light of her gift of clairvoyance, along with her rhizomatic identity as a *lwa-métis*—will apply the rotational movements of a Mozart sonata to the powers of his destiny, which is the work of interweaving the mostly tender experiences of life in society
> shuttles, steering wheels, hubs, wheels, pulleys, buckles, discs, windmills, paddles, and steam turbines of pretty ladies

---

* Mythical spirit, local god or evil genie, to which the Vodou faith attributes a fundamental role in Haiti's idiosyncrasy and historical escapades. During the experience of possession, or mystical trance, the *lwa* "mounts" the head of its "horse" (man or woman). The human being—thus invaded, possessed—is saddled and bridled to take what are often surrealist rides around Haiti's very real tragedy.

will help to trace, in his nomad's steps, the roots of the
royal banyan tree that the star of his elderly manhood will
need for traversing fields of tribulations, through the des-
erts and iniquities of a planetary era struggling with the
mystical missiles of barbarism. He will have to add all his
tribulations, existential reversals, psychological about-faces,
along with all he has achieved, to the well-tempered steel
of a poetic nomadism tormented by crossbars and succes-
sive sincerities. More than once—mamma mia!—covered
in scars, Dick Denizan, his head full-to-bursting with real-
utopia, threatened with the hijacking of his ideals, his fantasies adrift, his poeticizations at risk of death—more than
once Dianira Fontoriol's boy will have to unstitch himself
from the partisan cesspools of twentieth-century horror and
imposture, so to escape the traps of lawless mob mentalities,
of those who would seek to tamper with the story of his
tumultuous journey-vita

at each stopover in his marine animal's crossings, sor-
cerous State powers, erected along his path like so many
defilers of the humanities, will lay traps for him: both the
straight lines and the curves of his life will be caught up in
various battles—be it with switchblades or with rockets—
on behalf of a little prince of tenderness, compelled, in all
his innocence and compassion, to live in times of civil war,
within himself or with his fellow men, facing aggressions
from ancient dark forces—the sword, religion, and the market—the three orders that are at the origin of the shipwreck-
ing of the world

his Caribbean islander's tools will be those of the pirate
and the blacksmith: the hooks, grapples, pincers, bellows,
hammer, and anvil of the longtime adventurer. At the final
sun of his destiny, his vanquished poet's baraka will prevail,
despite everything, against fate, bad luck, and the countless
offenses to his appetite for life: at its peak, the state of possession that sustains his Popa Singer von Hofmannsthal will

be by his side to resist the cannibalistic geometry of whatever new ocean they try to make him cross. His wild race to the open sea will have to transport the gravel, the sand, the silt, and the marvelous plankton of childhood that protect the state of poetry from the murderous icebergs of hatred and barbarism . . .

# FIRST MOVEMENT

# 1

## A MONDAY THAT TURNS
## INTO TIGER PISS

I had not yet been conceived on that November afternoon when the young girl from Jacmel who would become my mother acquired a Singer sewing machine from a white import-exporter from Bord-de-Mer. A decade prior, this German businessman had fraudulently appropriated the name of an illustrious Austrian poet. One winter night in 1913, running from Emperor William II's justice, he had been compelled to flee Berlin. He had then boarded a Norwegian cargo ship in Hamburg and crossed the Atlantic with his patronymic booty in tow. That same year, he was to open up a trade in manufactured goods in a port town on the southeast coast of Haiti.

Exiting the shop that bore the name Hugo von Hofmannsthal (as my mother told me on more than one occasion), unable to find a porter, she had to contend with the bulky package containing her precious purchase. At that very moment, the man who would later become our papa Loulou passed by in his two-seater convertible. He cheekily offered to bring her home. They had known one another since adolescence. The well-known Jacmelian high life had given them multiple occasions on which to cross paths. They had played cards and dominos together. They had participated in kite-flying competitions. They had gotten tipsy on movement during carnival at the Excelsior Club's masked balls, or during those patronal feasts of Saint Philip and Saint James the Major that always got the whole town partying. They had also gone horseback riding and hiking, and taken dips in the Bassin-Bleu, at the Gosselin River, or on the beaches of Civadier and Carrefour-Raymond.

Up until then, it was mostly the group effect that had provided the underlying chemistry of their friendship. But it was the chance purchase at the faux von Hofsmannthal's shop that paved the way for their first tête-à-tête as a couple. Luc Denizan took full advantage of this windfall. He chose not to take the steep path up the coastline that led through the Bel Air plateau, less than ten minutes from Provence Street, straight to the Fontoriol residence. Instead, he took his horse for a meandering trot through the lower parts of Jacmel. He drove along Commerce and Saint-Anne Streets over to the maze of alleys in Bas-des-Orangers. After a detour through the Raquettes neighborhood, he headed hastily up Main Street and Cayes-Jacmel Avenue.

To protect the reputation of the virgin soon-to-be-bride, Denizan amused himself by telling some of the funniest stories of 1923. The innocent bursts of laughter that punctuated their little promenade precluded anything that would have smacked of a romantic intention. But then, once safely hidden behind the half-open Persian blinds of the Fontoriols' living room, the two young people completely neglected to unwrap the package they had set down on the rug. They didn't even touch the little sandwiches and chocolate snacks. They were entirely overcome by the promise smoldering between them: to ask that this love-born marriage raise them up into the time of a fruit-bearing tree-bed of yesteryear, several meters above the ground zero of life.

"Everything you've told me about those years," I said to my mother, "is easy to understand, other than that pseudonym with the overlong Germanic add-on you share with that sewing machine of yours. Why Popa Singer von Hofmannsthal? Why not just plain old 'Singer'—a well-enough-known brand? Can you imagine nicknaming your car L'il Roro *Ford* von Arnim Brentano? Or a soldier's rifle Bibi *Springfield* von Stauffenberg? I bet that aristocratic surname you picked is an expression of the same surge of tenderness that ended up turning Luc Denizan into the ephemeral Papa Loulou of our childhood."

"No, Dick, during your father's lifetime, neither I nor the Singer were known by this name, stolen from an elite Austrian literary genius. Thanks to the little shuttle perfected by the American inventor Isaac Singer in New York in 1851, a pharmacist and a seamstress from Jacmel were able to more or less make ends meet."

"But how did such a suitcase of a patronymic from a renowned white poet end up attached to a Mulatto housewife and the humble tool of her trade?"

"Well, that's just what happened. In 1937, on Good Friday morning, at the very beginning of my widowhood, one of my clients, the school headmistress Clariklé Thermosiris, who, like me, was well known for her dramatic states of spirit possession, hit me with the following oracle, in a flight of inspiration: 'Madame Loulou, beneath its sewing machine disguise, this machine of steel and wood enabling you to raise your five little orphans is controlled by a white papa-*lwa* originating from central Europe. Before its arrival in your sewing room, the Singer lived in steamy concubinage with a German businessman, a licensed identity thief. Out of that history, it has retained the power to crossbreed the plankton from the Great White European sea with the various substances suspended in the memory of the Negroes of the Americas: the terrifying crossing of the Atlantic Ocean, the ordeal of the cotton and sugar fields, Vodou rituals danced in the light of burning plantations, the agony of those who spent their entire lives in chains. Our Lady of the Thirty-Six Tribulations helps to manage the fallout from the colonial tragedy in a domestic sphere devoid of the rudder of a husband and father. Praise be to the spitting image of Madam Loulou! Praise be to Popa Singer von Hofmannsthal!'"

"Long live the Pietà of the Seven Sufferings of the Rainbow!" I said, so many years after that 1937 prophecy, as I stroked my mother's white hair.

A tiger-sized Haitian-style misfortune ended up making her existence a hypostasis of motherhood. She was venerated as a sort of multifaceted mother hen: beyond Déjanira or Dianira Fontoriol, she was also Madame Luc Denizan, for the public record; alias Mama Diani in local Haitian parlance; alias Madame Loulou, among the neighbors on Church Street in Jacmel. Beginning with that good omen of 1937, once in Port-au-Prince, she became known as Popa Singer von Hofmannsthal in the eyes of both her loved ones and her clientele. Her many forms of feminine being made for a profoundly rhizomatic identity beneath the patronymic borrowed from that Viennese magician of theater and poetry. Retain from now on, Ladies and Gentlemen gathered here, the (assumed?) name by which we have passionately loved the mama-*lwa* métis of our journey through the century. Hitched to the dire-straits nastiness of the rag trade, she sported the name proudly for her entire life, as much within the family as in those situations where she entered into communion with the mysteries of the mythical darkness of all Mothers!

It was also written that our creators would have both the necessary time and bustlings of solar love between their sheets to engender two daughters and three sons before death ate papa Luc's existence alive on the morning of October 20, 1936. From the moment of their father's passing, the rhythm of the Denizan brood was linked to the output of that sewing machine haunted by the ten fingers of a beneficent spirit fiercely compelled to do the hard labor that would keep the debacle of our childhood years from becoming an utter shipwreck.

What a Monday, March 22, 1958, that was! That morning, in the cottage garden adjoining the little house in Bourdon, my mother conjured up episodes from the Jacmelian past. The illuminating power that once captivated us in her evening storytelling exuded the same enchantment in broad daylight. Ever since my return from Europe, talking with her about our roots for a couple of hours each morning had been a ritual. In her mother-medium's memory, I nimbly made my way through the mythology of my maternal grandparents, Fontoriol and Fleuriblanc, and my paternal grandparents,

Denizan and Lafontant. Day after day in 1958, we made our way together beyond the family annals and up to the historical peak of our Creolacy. Roped together as mother and son, we scaled the walls of the "empty parentheses" of Haiti's history.

Everything began for us on the island of Hispaniola. One ordinary morning in 1515, the trade in Black flesh took over from the genocide of Arawak and Carib Indians. The following centuries were lived under the yoke of French and Spanish kings. The movement that upended their monarchical regimes, under the great mantle of universalization, was rather hostile to the humanization of the Black slaves. After the initial abolitionist measures of Robespierre's National Convention, Napoleonic power rushed to reestablish, throughout the Antilles, the chattel destiny inherited from the age of the Hapsburgs and the Bourbons. Only a *Black revolution* in Saint Domingue would be able to assure our passage from the *Black condition* to the human condition.

Nonetheless, the Haitians' decolonial miracle quickly turned into a nightmare: the constant taking up of arms and coups d'état, summary mass executions of innocent civilians, political massacres, volcanic eruptions of liberalism or of national smallpox, *bossale** Mardi Gras or Creole carnival—it all amounted to the same thing, like the po-tay-to po-tah-to of colonial times. Ever since the emancipatory gesture of 1804, without the slightest interruption, *Jacobin Negritude* has never ceased repeating the same pointless and interminable Haitianacy. Our historical hapax has left us at a hopeless standstill. Its cogwheels, more toothed than anywhere else, drunk with horror and desolation, turn endlessly in the emptiness of superstitious and slanderous fabulation.

"Our human adventure—miserere mei Deus to the very end, Dick—has a high coefficient of barbarism," my mother continued to lament. "We've somehow found a way to

---

* *Bossale* and *bossalerie* refer to the elements of African heritage that remained recalcitrant to the process of Créole hybridization.

discourage the mercy of Jesus Christ himself. That child of Bethlehem has forever distanced himself from the stench of beasts of prey that hovers over all our labors and all our days. The ferment of greenish froth that passes for our 'national' history makes little difference to the ruler of the valley of tears!"

"Ten years before you," I said to Mama Diani, "an Italian author wrote more or less the same thing about a desolate village on the southern part of the peninsula: 'Christ never came this far, nor did time, nor the individual soul, nor hope, nor the relation of cause to effect, nor reason nor history. . . . no message, human or divine, has reached this shadowy land, that knows neither sin nor redemption from sin . . .' My dear Popa, is it not Haiti's fate that Carlo Levi has described in his Italian fiction?"

"Except that for us, Dick, reality is a hundred times worse. On one never-before-seen day of storm and fire—Saturday, September 19, 1896, to be precise—three months before my fourth birthday, one year after the invention of the cinema, Christ arrived by sailboat at the mouth of the gulf of Jacmel. Instead of coming to the aid of the little town in flames, he chose instead to make an abrupt change of course. Without a second thought, after giving the finger to General Alphénix Ultimo and his victims, the white whale of redemption erased the latitudinal position of 'the-first-Black-republic-in-modern-history' from his navigational charts."

"The Redeemer was completely indifferent to the fact that General Ultimo, in the name of all Haitian citizens, then accused him of nonassistance to imperiled Black humanity?"

"Of course, Dick! Alas, it was the very least of his evangelical concerns. 'It can just go to hell, that SOS from the tribe of that paper general Alphénix!' That very afternoon, the First White Man in the history of humanity made an irreversible decision: to avoid at all costs bringing his infinite tenderness and compassion to the time and space of the Haitian people!"

"Could his Great Blessing have erased the effects of the parricide of October 1806?*"

"No, Dick, instead of cleansing our original sin, he made it so that the blackness of our skin has rubbed off on all the adventures of our endless tragedy."

"So Christ died on the cross for all human beings, but not for the tribes devouring one another on the cursed square miles of our volcanic hills."

"Yes, Dick, the facts are right there, in plain sight."

At that moment in the conversation a baritone voice brought my mother and me back from the flaming hilltops of nineteenth-century Jacmel to the atrocities of the time of Papa Doc that our country was then living through.

"Are we expecting someone?" asked Popa.

"Not to my knowledge."

"Excuse me, is anyone there?" insisted the visitor in the rough voice of a heavy rum drinker.

"Don't move, Dick," said Popa. "Let me go find out who it is."

She returned in a state of great agitation.

"The president's enormous car is parked just outside the house. An emissary from the Palace wants to speak to you. Monsieur Riphallus Foutu-Figaro, a real mouthful of a name, which he offered while kissing my hand like a true gentleman."

"Foutu-Figaro, for God's sake? Don't you mean Fonthus-Figaro? I had a classmate with that name, of course—back in the forties, at Pétion High School."

Indeed, Papa Doc's envoy was well and truly Rififo Fonthus-Figaro. From fourth grade all the way to our last year of high school, seated in the very last row of the classroom,

---

* In the late afternoon on October 17, 1806, father of Haitian Independence General Jean-Jacques Dessalines was assassinated by his own people in an ambush on the Pont-Rouge Bridge at the northern entrance to Port-au-Prince.

he and his hilarious antics were well known throughout the establishment on Montalais Street. Standing now in the door frame, thin and svelte in a navy blue suit, he was just about my height and my age. But his black felt Texas-style hat made him seem taller and older. Immediately after giving each other a hug, this descendant of my former high school companion bluntly said to me:

"You've been back in the country for three months, yet you've made no effort to meet the spiritual Leader-for-Life of the Nation-State. Your dear friend is very angry with you. It's my job to bring you to his Excellency by the scruff of your neck—that is, by force if necessary. Yes, Mister Wandering Black Man, the Great Electrifier of the Republic's cooches and pricks would like to chat—one-on-one, freely and forthwith, setting aside all matters of State—with the man he calls 'my poet-hero of the epic days of January 1946.' Take five seconds to doll yourself up Clark Gable–style. This Monday morning, March 22, the baraka that's about to pounce on the front of your pants is the spitting image of the naughty bits of one Miss Marilyn Monroe!"

"Well I'll be damned, Fifo! here you are, a talking cinema for Doc Duvalier—complete with the moving images and piano music for the job. Take a seat in that armchair. Popa will make us some real Jacmelian coffee."

Once Fonthus-Figaro was seated, he placed his wide-brimmed hat on a nearby chair and looked at it with an expression of veneration. Hands crossed on his knees, he began extolling its virtues.

"That's a deluxe Royal Stetson, a gift from our ambassador to the United Nations," he said, lowering his voice with a conspiratorial air, as if revealing some State secret that I would be ill advised to divulge.

"Indeed," I said, "that headgear of yours is impressive!"

"Can you believe, Richard Denizan," he insisted, lowering his voice even further, "that on any given day of the week a superdeluxe Son-Stet-Yal-Ro sits atop the head of Auntie Na's little boy? Now, that's one mother of a Texan hat! the same à la mode lid Sir Winston Churchill and Sir Anthony Eden are wearing in London, not to mention it's the one our compadre General Ike Eisenhower up in Washington wears when, in civilian dress, he takes that white dog of his starry empire out for a walk on the banks of the Potomac!"

"Pardon me, Fifo," I said, completely floored, as I escaped to the kitchen, "let's first have ourselves a little coffee with rum to celebrate our reunion."

My mother busied herself at the stove and with the porcelain coffee pot.

"What's going on?" she asked, distraught.

"If you can believe it, Popa, President Duvalier told Fonthus-Figaro that he wishes to 'chat—one-on-one, freely and forthwith, setting aside all matters of State—with the poet-hero of the epic days of January 1946.'"

"Miserere mei Deus! It's a trap, Dick. You can smell the tiger's genital double-zero from here!"

"Papa Doc is going to get a piece of my mind!"

"Be careful, Dick. Your old card-playing buddy disappeared long ago. You can never be too cautious these days: that *papacito* comes from assassins' stock. Even his Sunday nap reeks of the piss of wild animals."

"Well that predatory doc-doc is going to have to pick up the tab for some perfume!"

"And so, another Monday in this life turns into tiger piss!" sighed Popa, as someone known in Jacmel for her talent for communicating with the spirits of the future.

## 2

## HOMO PAPADOCUS

A limousine like this, with at least ten seats—well now, that gives a prose-dreamer something to work with! I nonetheless felt horribly disgusted to find myself in that car, solemnly traversing Port-au-Prince in the company of the President of the Republic's personal secretary. In the right corner of the backseat, spineless with shame, I was like a bag of dirty laundry, slouched over so as not to be recognized by passersby. In the other corner of the car, Fonthus-Figaro voluptuously displayed his self-satisfaction. We exchanged not a single word until reaching the Salon of Lost Steps in the National Palace.

"You'd think we were in the main hall of a train station at rush hour," I said.

"It's like this every God-given day. And, well, that's perfectly natural: any and everyone in Port-au-Prince wants a chance to feel—circulating through their own veins—the electric current that, right from this very spot, fuels the Negritude of all the Republic's cooches and pricks!"

Upon my arrival in his study, the Great Electrifier stood up and quickly came around his desk, headed in my direction. He peered at me on the sly at first. Once he'd sized me up, he hesitated for a moment before embracing me. He looked me in the eyes. He calculated my qualities and my defects. He had the wary and ceremonious expression of a doctor who worries that his diagnosis has somehow missed the case of typhus or a cancer of the large intestine.

"You are most welcome into the golden age of the Duvalierist revolution!" he said, in his confident falsetto.

His Excellency wore the exterior signs of some sort of great national mourning: a black flannel three-piece suit, a white bow tie with black dots, matching pocket square, and one-eyed glasses, the left eye hidden behind a dark lens. His overall appearance gave off a slyly aggressive and funereal air. The warmth of his welcome only made his State-terrorist getup seem that much darker. The Great Electrifier signaled to Fonthus-Figaro and to two others, a dapper captain and a secretary of agreeably uncertain age, that they should leave us alone.

"We've got quite a lot to talk about, haven't we, my dear Dick? Since our last tête-à-tête, rainwater has followed its course, though without always refreshing this humble country doctor's long walk through the desert. But now, here we are. My leadership in this kingdom has the rigor of an algebro-physiological formula: given Papa Doc and his Haitian-style-Black-power, what we have here, Dick, are two entities—$x$ and $y$. The vibration of the bossale $x$ must bring about the correlating vibration of the Creole $y$. This operation leads directly to a redefinition of the racial transcendence of the Negroes of Haiti. You get it, don't you? the theory of ethno-historico-cultural groupings that Lorimiro Bolant and I laid out back in the thirties in three little essays on bio-sociology. Since then, our youthful efforts have only become more significant in the eyes of the entire Caribbean scientific community: 'The Developments of a Generation,' 'Black Nation-State and Ethnic Cleansing,' 'The Class Problem Understood through the Epic of Haiti.'"

Deeply unsettled by this start to things, I had the foolish idea to try scratching the political beast's back by citing a passage from one of those three bits of nonsense I could still call to mind.

"*The axis of our action is constantly oriented toward an effort to detect the bio-psycho-algebraic elements of the Haitian man, so as to extract the substance of an ultra-nationalist doctrine from them . . .*"

"*. . . that, by anticipating the biological process of our identity, would quicken the quantic function indispensable to the ethnic purification of the island, thanks to the Vodou*

*National Salvation Front, which will be responsible for exalting and coordinating, in an organic Creole whole, the diverse sacred orders of human activity,"* Papa Doc continued, affecting his most learned tone. "Wasn't it just wonderful, codifying these eminently axiomatic values with the wildest totalitarian Pan-Negroism? The fellows that came up with that didn't have fifty years between the two of them, Dick, old fellow! Our methods come straight from the fire and the sword of political ideas. They'll enable us to build an ethnically pure country, historico-culturally cleansed of any white impurity and of any Mulatto stain: one Haiti, black like a Gothic oven or like the inside of an African leopard's mouth. We're founding a great nation, black like a crow's wing by dint of being molded by Lorimobolantian Duvalier-style black magic!"

"That's a long march that risks claiming many victims," I said, completely stunned.

"Joseph de Maistre is the authority on that front, notably in his *Evening in Saint-Petersburg.* You must have read this masterwork, of course, my dear poet, when you were at Sciences Politiques."

"Yes, Mr. President."

"None of this 'Mr. President' business between us, dear poet. Call me Doc Duvalier, like in the good old days when we used to play cards on Sunday afternoons on Eloy-Alfaro Street—you were precociously gifted at trois-sept. You were also a virtuosic titillator of clitorises among the many feminine muses of the Bas-Peu-de-Chose neighborhood! The future Papa Doc was always the big loser. You used to put clothespins on his nose, on the fleshy part of his forearm, in his hair, and on both his ears. And you'd proclaim your triumph at cards urbi et orbi. But back to my alter ego de Maistre: 'A political act is not judged by the number of victims it claims, but by the evils it prevents.' This you must recognize, first and foremost, as the primal faith and hope that motivates me, the first clinician of the Black race, fiercely determined to administer the penicillin of development to a republic infected by the Western hemisphere: in order to be spared great suffering, my Haitians must submit regularly to the rejuvenating treatment of the bloodbath!"

"Aside from de Maistre," I said, nearly speechless, "what might be some other inspirations for this mystical . . . seaside . . . terrorism?"

"Mystical seaside terrorism? Far from shocking me, I find your poetic phrase suits me perfectly well. To sum up, I'll cite a few off the top of my head: Mustafa Kemal Ataturk; Jacques Bénigne Bossuet, especially his Lenten sermons; Georges Jacques Danton, foremost Montagnard of the French Revolution; Emperor Faustin Soulouque the Magnificent; a pinch of Lévy-Bruhl for every Georges Sorel; the great Portuguese master Oliveira Salazar, of course; the Siamese brothers Marcel and André Boll; the fantastical Lorimo Bolant, my late brother in the applied ethnography of dictatorial politics; and, let us not forget, for the more discerning among us, the cream of the crop among the master thinkers of modern violence, last but not least, bloody-goddam! glory be to the incommensurable Islamo-Austrian Abderrahman von Baschmakoff!

"What's that you say, Your Excellency—sorry—Doc Duvalier?"

"My poor, dear comrade, have you never heard talk at the Sorbonne of the writings of von Baschmakoff? That giant of epistemology renewed the very foundations of political science as pertains to the role we must attribute in the history of civilizations to the particles of the ethno-mystical virus. I, your former card-playing buddy, possess the virtuosity of a veritable Paganini of State terrorism when he takes to his Stradivarius and executes the formidable Baschmakoffian musical scores that extract from the sacred violence of Vodou the cubic root of the identity of those American Negroes who remain faithful to the legendary Manes of Mother Africa!"

"So in your view, the ends always justify the means?"

"That shouldn't be surprising to a big-boy poet like yourself: absolute power fully sanctifies all tactics. Anyone looking for results can't get worked up about Papa Doc's hemato-*seaside* methods. That's the 'substantific marrow' of Duvalierist fundamentalism, the only doctrine suited to the suffering of this mini Nation-State. Must I really do the work of illuminating the poet's lantern?"

"Er, Mr. President, um, Doc Duvalier, for my humble part, I remain faithful to the democratic ideas my generation defended in *La Ruche,* at the end of the Second World War."

"The great new ideas of the young people of 1946—well, that's me! The beautiful libertarian youth of those days of *La Ruche,* it's Papa Doc—and no other Grand-Negro in power in the Caribbean—who incarnates them today. With international communism being illegal in Haiti, Duvalier-the-Great owes nothing to your friends in Moscow or Beijing. Abderrahman von Baschmakoff is the historical source of my legitimacy. In the realpolitik of the century, your Stalinism, imported from some cave in the Caucasus Mountains, is nothing more than a monk defrocked by the Russian Orthodox Church—the totalitarian product of a mustachioed Georgian, an exotic whitewash of a man whose doctrine has no future here. The tutelary spirit of the other Joe, the Frenchman Joseph de Maistre, comes to my rescue once again: 'There are insect predators, birds of prey and, of course, primate and bipedal predatory ideologies.' Like an active volcano, a predatory Negritude has been custom-tailored to serve the balls and the giant erections of the hemo-mystico-seaside terrorism of my dreams! My torrent of ethnic cleansing is a sacred papa-orgasm. It will propel the quanta of a goddam civilizing cosmico-libido-synergy right up modernity's cho-cho!"

"If you will, I hold a slightly less eruptive, less pornographic, and less blindly quantic view of Haiti's destiny . . ."

"Careful now, my rebellious old Jacmelian friend. Easy does it with whatever you're about to say. Don't be imprudent and start getting the Great Baron Samedi's* big-ole tits

---

* Vodou spirit, captain of cemeteries, androgynous prince of violent death, sultan of massacres.

heated up! Take heed not to rile up the endless hard-on of the papa of the arts, weapons, and laws of this here Black corner of the universe. Tucked into these pants there's a Great Negro Beast of Prey with the ferocity of a blue shark!"

"Tucked away in mine all you'll find is the tenderness of a good man."

"Don't get it in your head to oppose my program for liberation with a so-called tender sovereign good. You tell your buddies at the Kremlin: fired up like a mad dog, Super-Zozo-Duvalier is the greatest civilizer of the day. Don't end up with your poet's blood flowing in his gutters. Why don't you just focus instead on helping his quantic hard-on impregnate the totality of this ethno-Duvalierist civilization!"

I sat there, totally stupefied, in both body and spirit. The silence in the room could have been cut with an electric saw. Everything seemed to me more confusedly grim than when I arrived. I found myself face-to-face with a living offense to the Rights of Man and the Citizen. Homo Papadocus was right there, hands spread out flat on the black walnut of his desk. Just a few centimeters from his outspread fingers lay the dual symbol of his power: a Colt 45 placed on a Bible and a dagger resting on a copy of the Koran.

Papa Doc's eye was an active piranha in the aquarium of his tortoiseshell glasses. After a moment of indecision, faced with my bewilderment, the president suddenly took on the nasal intonations of a child's nursemaid, to soften the effect of the threats he had just made.

"I've known you since you were in short pants," he said. "You played barefoot in the dust on Eloy-Alfaro Street. I did a little Creole bamboula for the sparks of your first little booklet of poems. I fully embraced the fireworks from the time of *La Ruche*. I cared for you like a father that time you had malaria, brought back from a little sojourn among the mosquitos of Tortuga. You were my lucky partner in all those games of cards. The word in Port-au-Prince is that you're now something of a songbird happy in his love nest. Eternally blessed bastard, you scratch my back, and I'll scratch yours!"

"..."

"No later than last week," he began again, "my cousin Dodophe Bankoli-Klodestier, a fine connoisseur of Semitic flesh, confided in me that your wife, Madame Denizan, is a scandalously luminous specimen from head to toe. My dear friend, just what are you planning to do to ensure that her radiance is set up in comfortable conditions befitting her Judeo-Magyar origins? You can't be thinking to have that mad dog of the European Balkans live among the filth of Port-au-Prince's seedy neighborhoods, can you? If she is to keep up her champagne lifestyle, her Highness will need a villa furnished in the English style, cool and breezy in every season of the year of our Lord! To be protected from our heat waves, her chicness must enjoy the ideal temperature of the hills of Kenscoff or of Nouvelle Touraine. Only then will she be in any shape to play fugues or romantic sonatas on her siren's grand piano, on those moonlit nights for which Haiti is renowned all over the world."

In response to his lyrical flight, I said that Dito Sorel and I were well used to a frugal and studious life. We planned to dedicate ourselves to teaching private lessons; my wife spoke eight languages, and I was prepared to teach twentieth-century French literature. Turning our back on society life in Port-au-Prince, we would live modestly in the sunlight of our thousands of books.

He let out a sharp laugh, throwing his head back in his rocking chair.

"My dear little Mulatto, has exile really left you that far removed from our Creolacy? What private establishment these days would ever risk the two of you indoctrinating our precious youth with your empirico-critico-Leninism? And our allies from the US embassy? Do you really think the CIA recruited them for their capacity to remain indifferent to the danger of communist subversion a stone's throw from the shores of Florida? Only a humanism with the balls of a raging bull would ever employ a couple like you and your Carpathian polyglot beauty. So, to start, before naming you the head of our UN mission, what I've got in mind for your talents as a former student of Sciences Politiques is an important position in the Foreign Affairs Ministry. I can see you as director of the culture department. What do you say to my proposition?"

"I intend to remain faithful to the principles of my twenties," I said, laconically.

"Under the protection of your illustrious friend, all should go well for you here in Haiti. But without this Black man's green light . . ." He raised his arms heavenward. Eyes closed, he laid out in petto the fine mess I'd be in.

"In any case," he said, "there's no hurry. I'll happily give you a few days to consider all of this carefully. One of these evenings, you and Dracula's great-niece will come dine at the Palace. Madame Simone Duvalier will be delighted to receive the Denizans. In the meantime, I have a surprise for you."

He pressed a button. A high-ranking officer appeared, followed by a boy carrying three glasses of champagne on a tray. I recognized the man as General Antonio Th. Kébreau, the chief of staff of the armed forces, the man responsible for the reprisals against the main shantytown in Port-au-Prince. The people of La Saline had shown too little enthusiasm for Candidate Duvalier's campaign for his taste. He left more than a thousand people dead in that neighborhood, mostly women and children stabbed to death in their sleep. That massacre ended up opening the way to the "electoral heist" of September 22, 1957.

The executor of Duvalier's great works, rakish and cheerful, came toward me. He effusively took both of my hands in his.

"Welcome! I'm so happy to see you back among us safe and sound."

"Ah! General Tonio," said Duvalier, "you remember the poet-hero of the general strike of January 1946? Back in those days, out in the streets of Port-au-Prince, hordes of young people were making life pretty difficult for the authority of a certain Captain Kébreau . . . Exile appears to have rusted his anarchist cleric's machete. Today, the author of *Étincelles* joins the valiant cohort of the Vodou National Salvation Front of his own free Negro will!"

"Heartfelt congratulations, Mr. President! Let's drink to that."

"A quality recruit, isn't he, General Tonio? Our Duvaliero-nationalist Dick has let go of that white man's Judeo-Bolshevism. We must celebrate his return to the cradle of his native land!"

# 3

## COMRADE KOLA

That same Monday, March 22, 1958, in the early evening, in a secret location in Port-au-Prince, I was meant to meet with the Secretary General of the Haitian Communist Party. After the conversation with Papa Doc-Abderrahman, fearful of being tailed by his Gestapo, I tried vainly to cancel the rendezvous. By attending would I not be endangering a splinter group that was just taking its first painful steps into the world of clandestinity? But did I not have the duty to inform my comrades as quickly as possible about my interview with the dictator?

After a few clever detours through the obscurity of the back alleys of Bas-Peu-de-Choses, I arrived on the stroke of eight o'clock at the address that had been passed to me the previous evening by the dentist, who was my contact man. I stumbled blindly along a dirt passageway leading to the interior courtyard of a wooden house. The gallery railings had been assembled crookedly, with no semblance of order. An elderly man stood waiting for me in the half-open doorway. He gave a sign to follow him. Hanging on the wall of the room, a small kerosene lamp weakly illuminated the spare furnishings—three straw chairs and a cot.

"Good evening, Comrade Koka," he said, smiling. "Comrade Kola shouldn't be much longer."

In Paris, before going to board a cargo ship to Rotterdam, I'd been warned that I'd have a fake name in Haiti. It would sound like the first two syllables of a popular soft drink. But it would be spelled Haitian style, that is, with *k* rather than *c:* Koka. In the bewitching context of créolité, that could be the name of some sort of toddy-elixir: it would make you live more intensely or—conversely—it would forever zombify your poor soul: magisterial bringer of wild hope for rejuvenation or zombifying brew. Less than a minute after I'd had that amusing thought, a *grimaud*\* in his thirties entered on tiptoe through a hidden door.

"Hello, Mr. Koka," he said. His throaty voice was as lugubriously affected as his plainclothes Haitian cop getup.

"Good evening, Comrade Kola," I said.

"I'm not Comrade Kola," he said. "You've got the wrong man. The wrong Party altogether," he continued, self-importantly. "This afternoon, the Party learned from a reputable source that you were President Duvalier's guest at the National Palace. On getting this news, the Party executives decided not to risk the safety of our leader. I've been sent in Comrade Kola's place solely to hear the explanation you owe the Party regarding this morning's scandalous meeting."

"Come now, comrade, let's not make a big fuss about this."

"Why is it that, since your arrival, you've hidden from the Party your connection with the number one adversary of this country's workers?

"The explanation is simple: a dozen or so years ago, before the events of 1946 I was mixed up in, Doc Duvalier and I were neighbors. In fact, we lived right around here. We were on close terms. We played cards together regularly. One night, when I was eighteen years old, I was stricken with a life-threatening bout of malaria. Doc Duvalier had me admitted to the general hospital, in the private ward where he was the head physician. For an entire month he entrusted me to the gentle ministrations of a nurse sent straight from heaven. Gabriela ended up curing both my red blood cells and the turmoil of my postadolescence. At the end of this doubly redeeming treatment, the good doctor would hear no talk of payment. 'Popa's Singer sewing machine has other fish to fry.' How could I spit on his outpouring of generosity? How could I forget, hail-Mary-full-of-grace, the angel Gabriela,

---

\* A Haitian with fair skin and abundant kinky hair.

sent night after night by the doctor Duvalier of 1946 to treat my contaminated blood? Urgently summoned to the presidential palace, I unthinkingly agreed to go there accompanied by someone I'd known since my days at Pétion High School."

"That's exactly what's scandalous about this: all of Port-au-Prince saw you pass by in the tyrant's Cadillac, seated right next to Fonthus-Figaro. You stayed there all alone with the enemy of our class. You popped a bottle of Veuve Clicquot with him, in the presence of the assassin Kébreau. Then that gangster of all our misfortunes ostentatiously escorted you back to Bourdon. The day's *télédyòl** has already pegged you as a full-on Tonton Macoute of the cultural realm!"

"I may have been seated at the devil's table, but I was holding a long spoon. Truthfully, there's nothing to get so worked up about, Comrade Kola—oh, sorry!—Comrade, what's your name again? With whom do I have the honor of speaking?"

"That's not important, Mister Koka. You can call me Comrade Baron Samedi, if you'd like, so as not to upset your powerful friends."

"Let's go with Comrade Baron Samedi, then! You know as well as I do that the *télédyòl* is the only communication service that works around here. Our third of an island is a raging megalomaniac. Every one of us is subject to its mudslinging fabrications. I, too, am subject to the common fate. That being said, this evening, several very real facts attest to my integrity. First of all, I unequivocally refused our adversaries' offer to join their ranks. Second, I bring to the Party a firsthand account of the doings of our Black Führer, who, as of now, is the incarnation of radical evil. I witnessed him threaten to implement the zombification of all life in Haiti. Doc Duvalier has exchanged the caduceus for the swastika!"

---

* From the Greek *tēle*, "at a distance," and the Haitian *dyòl*, "mouth." It refers, then, to a mode of word-of-mouth. In its most hallucinatory form, it serves as oral support for the existential standstill around which the "endless tragedy" of the Haitian people turns.

"That point of view is completely false. Duvalier is a pathetic little straw homunculus. His nationalist Duvalierism is nothing more than a bunch of cock-and-bull blah-blah-blah. His fundamentalist Pan-Negroism won't last long. In effect, the days of your pocket-sized Hitler Abderrahman are numbered. The real danger isn't that *bande-rara*\* caliph. We'd do better to fear his gun-toting right-hand man, the butcher-cop of La Saline, General Kébreau. His coup-d'état is imminent."

"That's not the impression I got observing the complicity of those two long-term buddies. The Party will one day regret having underestimated the ordeal Papa Doc is preparing for us."

"You have some nerve giving lessons in strategy to the enlightened leaders of the Party! Why don't you start by clearing yourself of the accusation that you're sharing intelligence with our class enemy. You've been discredited in the eyes of the national and international proletariat. Before entrusting you with even the slightest leadership task, our regulatory committee expects a detailed biography from you."

"A what, Comrade Kola?"

"A detailed bio-gra-phic-al report. Explain to the Party how your stone rolled among the Great Whites during the Cold War! That will be all for tonight, Mister Koka!"

With these words, without saying good-bye, the Baron Samedi of the Cominform slipped out into the anthropophagic darkness of Port-au-Prince.

---

\* A group of rural carnival musicians, very popular in Haiti.

# A RETURN TO HAITI

In the pages of the December 15–31, 1957, edition (no. 2, vol. 1) of the *Coumbite* gazette, Dianira Fontoriol, also known by the name Popa Singer von Hofmannsthal, grabbed her pen case and some of that violet ink one used to write with back in the olden days, to welcome her son Dick:

our hills rejoice at the good news of your feet on my doorstep, joyful those lucky messenger's feetfirst of yours, Bourdon rejoices at your hot-blooded breaking of the day into the flaming time and space of Dito, your white treasure of a garden-woman, joyful are that beaver and that panpipe ready to forge the great libertarian sun of your orgasm under the roof a mother doubly overjoyed by the solar celebration of a return to Port-au-Prince

we have missed you, my son: for you, to speak of Popa Singer from afar was to speak of your lost third of an island: with words of elsewhere your banyan roots grew strong on the chessboard of the Cold War, bringer of the August 29 of your thirtieth birthday miserere mei Deus where your twenty-first year passed into a sleepless night

I never knew your rebellious and sporting years, nor did I know the time of your libertine and studious pursuits, owed to the kindness of the international student dorms at the University of Paris. You didn't have Popa Singer's tenderness by your side to protect you from the snowstorms and the frigid autumn winds, and from the werewolf-gray sidewalks where, I'm told, the feline incivility of "White" people

at times lays out panther traps for students of the so-called
Black race

far away from here, where the sorcerers of the so-called
white race reside, you hopped on the moving train of those
years of apprenticeship in the ways of the world: where did
it go, your twenty-fifth year spent in Prague and in Moscow,
precociously dismayed in the face of the approaching shipwreck of the utopias of your youth, stolen away from me;
your days spent sheltered behind an iron curtain where the
very DNA of brotherly coexistence dissipated into toxic fumes

you'd have had a devil of a time finding a bamboo frame,
some paper, and enough wind to launch—into the azure of
the humanities—the words of a child on the verge of tears
who marvels at relearning tenderness and at the great good
that roaring with laughter can do. The kite of old age must
be prepared for flight well in advance: faced with the impos-
sibility of returning to the past, it must rise up without getting lost in the clouds. Soaring without a string, there'd be
no room for missing your shot, stirred up by the fire of your
being, until the very zenith where the Indian summer of your
creations transforms the aged chaos of the Haitian night into
a cinema of the dawn, in the Frenchified sunshine of dreams
and the tragically true stories of an entire lifetime.

# SECOND MOVEMENT

# 4

## POPA SINGER
## VON HOFMANNSTHAL'S UTOPIA

Back at the house in Bourdon, I recounted nothing—neither to my mother nor to my companion Dito—of the substance of the conversations I'd had that morning—from the extreme right—with the real-life Baron Samedi of Black power, or that evening—from the extreme left—with the real-life "red" Baron Samedi of the October Revolution. Thinking about it more than forty years later, I still lower my head in shame and indignation. Back in those days, Dito had her own cross to bear: far from her family in Israel, she was caught in the trap of a regime that was the inverse of the Hebrew Middle Eastern nation. She needed time to get used to the *Haitianas-series* of her adoptive land.

During Sunday lunch on March 28, 1958, with the whole family gathered around our mother Popa, I was equally evasive. My brothers and sisters, along with my two brothers-in-law, tried in vain to extract from me the keys for decoding the *télédyòl* that had circulated throughout Port-au-Prince on the subject of my civic behavior, all day on that Monday the 22nd.

"Sure, there's plenty to chew on in all that made-up nonsense," I said. "But neither the devil nor the good Lord will find what they're looking for. One thing is certain: after my meeting with the president, there's no way I'm going along with his plan for me to join the Vodou National Salvation Front."

As for the events that had preceded our return to the country, Dito and I had front-row seats. Our relatives squabbled endlessly about the smallest details of the preceding months. The various adventures leading up to Papa Doc's 1957 electoral heist, which he'd pulled off thanks to the support of

General Kébreau, made up a puzzle that they never stopped trying to piece together. Régis, my youngest brother, a twenty-eight-year-old lawyer, had been an adviser to the candidate Marc-Antoine Grandet, a former minister of finance whom he believed to be both sincerely democratic and wise. Rachid Ben Estefano, my sister Rita's spouse, was a Middle Eastern shopkeeper. He swore by the ex-senator Louis Delajoie, an industrialist reputed for his reinforced-concrete–style liberal dandyism. Didier Jeannotin, my sister Lucie's husband, who taught Greek at Louverture High School, admitted to being "a dyed-in-the-wool Duvalierist from the very beginning." Guy-Luc, my younger brother, was more than anything else a propolis and royal jelly enthusiast. His beekeeper's propheti-cism would have inclined him to vote for Daniel Fignotardif, populist before his time, had the environmentalist leader's candidacy not been nullified at the last moment. As for Popa, her clairvoyance had been unable to make heads or tails of the muddle of partisan passions gathered under her roof.

"My household is always on the verge of imploding," she lamented.

For months, in an effort to stay out of it, she either con-strained herself to the role of arbiter or attempted to divert her progeny's attention toward some enigmatic fancy meant to distract them from their quarrels.

"If I were to propose a political program to the citizenry," she asked that Sunday, "guess which one I'd be leaning toward?"

"You'd be a high-powered Christian Democrat," said Rita.

"Admit it, Rita, you don't know mama very well."

"Consistent with your favorite pastime—having multiple irons in the fire—you'd serve both Christ and the gods of Vodou," said Lucie.

"Where matters of faith are concerned you may be right, Cici. But when it comes to the civic arena, it's not the same thing at all."

My Bedouin brother-in-law then threw a handful of Arabian desert sand into my garden.

"Unlike Dick," he said, "you wouldn't be indifferent to the Word of the Prophet. As is conducive to the Koran, the strength of your leniency and mercy would be in harmony with the wrath of a leader of a holy war. I can easily see you at the head of a thunderous jihad, fighting to stop Haiti's race into the abyss!"

"You're wrong, Rachid—and by a long shot! I loathe any dogma of extermination. Extremist fundamentalism will never be my cup of ginger tea. Cat got your tongues?"

"Yes-s-s-s," the entire household cried to the heavens.

"The truth is, children, I would be neither Papa-Doc-ist, nor Bolshevik, nor jihadist off to war in the name of some barbaric divinity. For me, politics would be the art of bringing each member of our species into brotherly harmony with the stirrings of life. Not having any greater means of resistance than a Singer sewing machine, I'd be a diehard Singerocrat . . ."

Guy-Luc couldn't resist a play on words.

"You'd end up being paid no more than a *song*, like every other victim of a political party."

"Come now, Guy-Luc, with *Popa-style democratic Singerism*, all citizens would be infused with the passion of a shared panhumanism, rather than any partisan spirit. The mere fact of existing would amaze them to the point of ecstasy. The rudiments of this amazement would be to live in a society that keeps them safe and warm in proximity to their neighbor. Before any idea of civic life, any ideological or religious choice, the fact of living together on the land of our fathers would be linked as profoundly to the most innocent subjects as to the grandest aspirations: the flight of butterflies / the soaring flights of the human heart; the gentle course of a stream in the sunlight / the swells of brotherly spirit in the countryside; a woman's periodic bloody flow / the silence that persists in the sounds of the sea . . ."

"Bravo!" cried Rachid, "Mama Popa is as much of a poet as her eldest son!"

"There are," our mother continued, "many other phenomena as simple as a hello. They're what allow us to perceive both joy and suffering, life and death, time and eternity within the same flash of truth. The headiness of living together on this third of an island is guaranteed to us gratis pro Deo, thank you very much: a mango tree dotted with flowers in the morning, the dove's lament at dusk, a pair of hummingbirds resting in their nest under the light of the moon, a horse enraptured by his midday tuft of grass, the little boy who believes all you have to do is raise a kite in someone else's sky in order to wipe out the wrongs done to the idea of brotherhood among members of the many humanities found in every corner of the planet."

"Hosanna!" cried Dito, "Mama Popa is a much better poet than her son!"

"Go ahead," said Guy-Luc, "tell us more about your utopia."

"My idea of *Singerist civility* would help even the most utterly defeated people, as we are today, to defy the mystical hatreds and barbaric missiles of the past. The art of being together in *panhumanity* would have the same solar appeal as, who knows, the aroma and the flavor of warm bread, the taste of the food and drink we share with the good Lord on this peaceful Sunday. Faced with the raging iniquity of our global leaders, to defeat the vast, toothy mechanism of History means being able to freely bring together around the same familial table a Jewish daughter-in-law and a Palestinian son-in-law in shared celebration of the poetry of a Haitian mother with the pen name Popa Singer von Hofmannsthal. My utopia, if you will, Guy-Luc, would be to extract the tenderness and beauty of the propolis of democratic life to revitalize within the beehive of our common humanity—miserere mei Deus!—our values and our tattered sense of the marvelous!"

"Praise be Popa Singer's utopia! May all power be in the hands of von Hofmannsthal!" I cried, amid the cheers and bursts of laughter of all the guests at our Sunday table.

On that afternoon at the end of March 1958, Mama Popa succeeded in keeping at bay the quarrels that so often left a taste of cold ashes in our mouths.

# 5

## FAIRYTALE OF THE AUGEAN STABLES

Less than a week later, on the night of April 7–8, 1958, we had all gone to bed early. After a stifling day, the trade winds from the Gulf of Gonâve had released a waterfall of cool rain in the skies of Port-au-Prince. Their rhythm had granted us an initial phase of sleep filled with placid dreams. It was jarringly interrupted by a nightmarish commotion: someone was knocking furiously on all the doors and windows of the house at once.

"Police! Open up in the name of the law, damn it!"

We gathered in the living room to confront the Tonton Macoutes. I made my way toward the front door. My mother authoritatively pushed me aside.

"Let me greet these barbarians," she said.

A vicious shove immediately thrust her back into our arms. A dozen or so men, some of them in plainclothes—fedoras, black sunglasses—some in police khakis, foaming at the mouth, pushed their way into our home.

"Ladies-and-gentlemen-of-Mulatto-society, hands in the air goddammit! The NSV* have arrived!"

In the same way that some of us are born to be soccer or rugby players, the militiamen and police officers of the armed forces seemed to have been built, head to toe, for the task of perpetrating the sort of nocturnal violence they were carrying out right then.

---

* Volontaires de la sécurité nationale (National Security Volunteers), official name for Duvalier's political police force, better known by the folkloric name Tontons Macoutes, Creole equivalent of the Bogeyman, whose criminal behavior is that of a tropical Nazi SS.

Their presence in the house gave off a scent of savage energy. Their swaggering and aggressive demeanor conformed perfectly with their tenth-rate musculature. The various weapons they carried (Colt 45, rifle, machine gun, machete, hatchet, ax, iron-cutting shears) seemed like additional muscles, swollen with the vital force they deployed for the all-out destruction of others.

The captain who was giving the orders immediately took me aside.

"You and the white lady, you were invited to dine at the Palace. Our Spiritual Leader and Mama Simone waited for you in vain all evening. That amounts to a casus belli as far as we're concerned."

"My son knows his manners, Captain," said Popa. "Two days ago, he politely apologized for not being able to accept the presidential couple's flattering invitation."

"Madam," said the officer, "your words are worth nothing here. Let's hear from your schemer of a son, and keep your hands in the air, damn it!"

"These days," I said, "my wife is obliged to stay in her room. She's not well. And so we couldn't go out into the city. I spoke with the chief of protocol on the phone yesterday. He formally promised to communicate our regrets to the President and First Lady of the Republic."

"We wouldn't have put together a full police operation tonight if it were only a matter of a breach of etiquette vis-à-vis the Palace. Your overall conduct undermines the safety of the State. We have orders to take a look at your secret associates. Where do you keep your books?"

"Where, goddammit, are your Augean stables?" added the plainclothed head of the militiamen.

"First of all, Captain," I said, "let me see your warrant."

In response to my question, the man in khakis turned and beckoned to his squad.

"Take a look, my friends: we're being perfectly polite with this citizen. He still has all thirty-two of his teeth and his set of passion fruit. And he thanks us by throwing big words he learned hanging out with those white folks at the Sorbonne in our faces. Mister Sorbonne has the nerve to ask us for a warrant!"

"Where the hell is that Augean pigsty? Where are those goddamn giant-pig-books of yours?" interrupted the head Macoute again, drawing his Colt 45.

"There are nothing but fairytales in my son's library," said Popa. (A week before, on the alert ever since the terrible Kima-Rimini Affair,* her foresight had led us to entrust an elderly aunt in Jacmel with hundreds of works that risked being deemed "subversive.")

"Madam," said the head Macoute, placing his weapon against the nape of my mother's neck, "are you or are you not going to shut your Mardi Gras *dyol* of a mouth?"

"You don't scare me, you know," said Popa. "Get your devil-gun away from me . . ." (My mother confirmed the next morning that she'd been about to slap her aggressor in the face.)

"Come this way," I said just in time, to avoid a massacre.

Our bedroom was covered with books, from floor to ceiling.

"Well, well then!" exclaimed the assailants in unison.

They found themselves in possession of more incriminating evidence than they needed to back up the charge of "flagrant attack on the security of the State."

The hunt for "suspicious" works went on into the early hours of the morning. Popa in her nightgown, Dito in her bathrobe, Guy-Luc and I in pajamas, our brother Régis in his underwear—we were piled up in the back of the room, arms raised, threatened by the Colt 45, Springfield rifles, and

---

* One night in mid-February 1958, masked intruders invaded the home of Yvonne Kima-Rimini, editor of *Haïti-Miroir,* an important opposition journal. A divorcée, Madame Kima-Rimini and her two daughters (eighteen-year-old Mona, sixteen-year-old Lisa) were abducted and brought to a deserted trail in the Frères District, where they were brutally raped and murdered.

Thompson machine guns, not to mention all those sharp-edged weapons. Standing up or perched on chairs, the men assisted the captain and head Macoute as they inspected the many titles in our library.

A corporal, after looking over a leather-bound copy of Stendhal with disgust, said aloud:

"*The Red and the Black,* Captain?"

"Explosive materials, Corporal Milord, pack it up!"

"*War and Peace,* Captain?"

"Another stick of dynamite, Sergeant Grandgosier."

"*Darkness at Noon,* Captain?"

"A compendium of general chronometry. You've earned a zero for that question, you dunce of a militiaman!"

"*The Heart Is a Lonely Hunter,* Captain?"

"Any heart armed with a hunting rifle falls ipso facto within the domain of the law. Pack it up, goddammit!"

"*Little Red Riding Hood,* Captain?"

"An agitator who pins Bolshevik ideas to her straw hat. To the paddy wagon!"

"*The Little Prince,* Captain?"

"An evildoer who began conspiring from the cradle," said the head militiaman, in the place of the captain.

"*A Farewell to Arms,* Captain?"

"A misdemeanor charge for illegally bearing a weapon of war! Before the farewell there had to be a hello to those arms! Pack it up!"

"*The White-Haired Revolver,* Captain?"

"An M2 Browning disguised as an old man is still an automatic weapon!"

"*Miraculous Weapons,* Captain?"

"Another piece of incriminating evidence to collect! It's a case of arms trafficking!"

"*Pablo Picasso,* Captain?"

"A goddamn *pickax* oh! Pack it up, no questions asked!"

For two hours we listened to the burlesque litany of "sonofabitch holy war manuals" that had to be "taken out of commission." In less lugubrious circumstances we'd all have burst out laughing every time. Only Popa took the risk, in the case of the Spanish painter, of expressing herself plainly.

"That man's weapon is a paintbrush," she said. "Pablo Picasso is the greatest artist of the century. In *requisitioning* it, Captain, you're desecrating the beauty of the world itself!"

"Shut your giant calabash-*dyol*, werewolf-lady!" said the head militiaman. "A last name like that can only be a white threat to the sainted Duvalierian order! Down with Don Pablo and his pickax, oh!"

Their mission accomplished, the captain counted the hundred or so books, folktales, essays, poetry collections, dictionaries, grammar books, and biographies of famous persons that would finish their days in a great literary bonfire. He put together several batches, which he distributed among his men. He then graced us with a merciless word of caution.

"The cleaning out of your stables this evening was a generous warning from the Great-Electrifier-Spiritual-Leader to an ungrateful false friend. Should we have to come back, you won't be dealing with a cadet trained at West Point. He has treated you fairly well. The next time, you'll be at the mercy of that dashing plainclothed mass of muscles," he said, pointing at the Tonton Macoutes.

"And my boys don't speak French," said the head militiaman. "They haven't been to the Sorbonne. They'll have you listening to some truly fiery Creole!"

The captain went down the steps of the house and then turned to me abruptly.

"I almost forgot to tell you, Master Augeas, the chief of police Colonel Marcel Marcellus expects you this afternoon at our headquarters on the Champs-de-Mars, at exactly four o'clock, for a follow-up inquiry into this ongoing judicial matter."

# 6

## DEATH MADE TO MEASURE

Guess who was on front desk duty at police headquarters that afternoon? My cousin, First Lieutenant Leslie Fontoriol, the youngest of my uncle Hans's fifteen children. The eldest girl, Célina, was the angel of my adolescence. From 1937 to 1940, as I mourned my father, Lili embodied the consolation of happy vacation days up in the hills that tumbled down to the foamy coastline of the gulf of Jacmel. After so many years spent far away from her green eyes, being welcomed in a place like that by one of her brothers boded well.

"I'm well aware of your troubles, dear Dick," said my cousin in a low voice. "Colonel Marcellus is waiting for you. He's a good guy, you know, as long as there's no police chief breathing down his neck. Like all of us here at the station, he's terrified by that mercenary. But in the company of the lower-ranking squad members he's more submissive than a second-class officer. If it's only him receiving you, everything will be just fine. Chaperoned by another Macoute, he'll be playing his role as poet-breaker to the hilt. I'll bring you up to his floor."

"Tell me how Lili's doing, I said as we went up the stairs. I desperately long to see Uncle Hans, Aunt Frida, and—ave Maria!—Lili again! After our dips in the sea on those dreamy afternoons the whole crew used to rinse off in the waterfall of a mountain stream. Lili and I, we were always the last ones to make it back home, completely out of breath."

"Lili's expecting her fifth child. She'll maybe have ten more like our mother. In Jacmel, my sister never stops talking about you: she always links the story of those vacations at Meyer Beach to some mysterious 'third bank of the river' . . ."

We'd arrived at Colonel Marcellus's door. Leslie knocked on it lightly.

"Come in!" said a commanding voice.

I went in before my cousin. The colonel wasn't alone. To his right was seated a middle-aged civilian. The man looked elegant in a very becoming navy blue suit, clearly a British cut. He didn't even deign to get up, as the colonel had so courteously done to greet my arrival.

Leslie stood at attention, complete with heel-clacking.

"Mr. Richard Denizan, Colonel. The writer you summoned."

"Thank you, Lieutenant. At ease!"

At the moment of his about-face, I caught a flash of anxiety in Leslie's gray-green gaze. In my incorrigible romanticism, I immediately saw in it a reflection of the marvelous days of Lili.

"Take a seat," said the colonel, indicating a mahogany armchair. "His Excellency Clovis Barbotog, commander of the NSV, insisted on joining this conversation I wanted to have with you after what happened last night at your home in Bourdon."

"So then, Comrade," interjected Barbotog unceremoniously, "we have the nerve to insult the proverbial generosity of the Great Electrifier of the Loins and Souls of the Republic? Rather than accept the honor of dining at the table of the glorious presidential couple of this nation we prefer conspiring with white foreign authors?"

" . . ."

"The overwhelming proof of your plot against the security of the state is all right here," he said, pivoting toward an adjoining table on which all the books taken from my home several hours earlier had been stacked.

"Come now, Mr. Barbotog . . ."

"That's 'Excellency,' thank you very much," interrupted the colonel.

"Your Excellency," I began again, "do you truly believe that Li Po, Shakespeare, Mozart, Saadi, Omar Khayyam, Flaubert,

Tolstoy, Ibsen, Selma Lagerlöf, Pirandello, Carson McCullers, Joyce, Borges, Pavese, Neruda, Pablo Picasso would be giving lessons in conspiracy to a humble Haitian poet?"

"Perhaps they've all got better things to do. But here in your library, who'd be willing to vouch for all the disgusting, high-falutin' whites keeping you company day and night?" he asked, glancing suspiciously at the stacks of books.

After a brief hesitation, he stood up and grabbed a book from the pile.

"I hit the bull's-eye! *The Heart Is a Lonely Hunter.* I have no idea what tale Madame McCullers is telling here. But I'm sure of one thing, as is Colonel Marcellus: it's not about chasing butterflies. An angry hunter is what you were at age nineteen. You're the one who started up that goddamned national strike in the streets of Port-au-Prince. Back in 1946, that rag of yours, *La Ruche,* was behind the anarchist uprising of young people that toppled President Elie Lescot. Lonely? Is that not what you are, after twelve years of wandering around white people's countries? We never see you here in town. All our special services are aware: the Bolsheviks are plotting in the shadows. Dark, humid spaces are ideal for the Reds to do their work of undermining."

"To hear Your Excellency tell it, we'd be more inclined to shout: Pill bugs of the world, unite!" (I immediately regretted saying it.)

"*Exactement,* my little cherry-balled, Marx-loving comrade. You belong to the race of nocturnal orthoptera: pill bugs, water bugs, arthropods, cockroaches, and other disgusting first-order insect *vermin,* a motley collection of pathetic extreme-Left *kafirs** that we must crush under our heel, just like this!" he said, slamming the floor with his left foot.

"Mr. Denizan," interjected the colonel suavely, "there's one thing that's bothering our office more than anything else: how are you and Mrs. Denizan planning to make a decent living here in Haiti?"

---

* Arabic word meaning miscreant, infidel, renegade.

"Congratulations, Colonel," said Barbotog. "A very good question, very important, of course," he emphasized, looking straight into my eyes. "Other than love and tropical rainwater, how do you mean to afford a situation suitable for Miss Denizan's Judeo-Christian sex appeal?"

"My wife and I taught foreign languages in São Paulo and Rio de Janeiro. Why wouldn't we do the same in our country?"

"You can forget about any teaching you may have done in Brazil, goddammit! The President has already warned you about this. Colonel Marcellus and I, following the example of our spiritual leader, are merciless when it comes to protecting the unsophisticated people of the revolution from the virus of Marxism."

"We also have experience with journalism, which we acquired in Paris and South America. We plan to publish pieces on literature, the visual arts, and music and film history in the newspapers here."

"Colonel Marcellus, draw a big fat Baron Samedi cross straight through Madame Denizan and her agitator of a husband's idea of publishing pseudoartistic essays. Those two aren't journalists anymore, and that's goddamn final! All opinions are at the mercy of our censors, isn't that right, Colonel?"

"Of course, Excellency. In addition to the radio, we keep the written press, the *télédyòl*, the political and domestic *tripotages*,* and all word-of-mouth communication in our sights, day and night. After all the gossip surrounding that Kima-Rimini business, all that's left to do is to bring to heel that *tripote*-slinging handful of columnists still puffing out their chests in the pages of *Haïti-Miroir, Le Patriote, Coumbite,* and *Le Petit Matin du vendredi* . . .

---

* In people's private carnivals, this form of media picks up where the *télédyòl* leaves off. Its "rumor-has-it" gives rise to quotidian oneirico-picaresque entanglements.

"What's keeping our boys of the NSV from bringing those doctors of fucking François Mauriac–speak down a peg or two?

"If you slam every door in our face," I said, "we'll leave. Sometimes exile can be a fine vocation."

"The Judeo-French half is free to go back to Paris or Jerusalem. That's what I'd do if I were her. The fate of her beauty is at stake. From what they're saying in Port-au-Prince, she's a credit to her race. As for you, tiny-eared-l'il-Mulatto from Jacmel, here you are—caught in the trap of your native land. You'll need an exit visa on your Haitian passport. After the flagrant casus belli of last night, are you sure you'll be able to get one?"

" . . ."

"There is, perhaps," said the colonel, "one other possibility: a very personal letter of goodwill addressed to the president. Your pen will likely be capable of formulating a few words of contrition. Doctor Duvalier isn't one to let a friend who's properly repented go down in flames. Isn't that right, Excellency?"

"Indeed, halfway between the Tarpeian Rock and the Capitol, one might still blow away the fumes of destiny. Not far from here, at the Temple of Jupiter, Duvalierist good fortune still might be willing to coddle those two orphans hidden away in your underpants. It might even transform them from their state of slumber into the joyfully ringing bells of the Virgin Mary! To that end, I'll take you in my car. We'll surprise Doc Duvalier. I can imagine how pleased our spiritual leader will be to let bygones be bygones vis-à-vis the dubious company you've been keeping." (Angry glance at the Carson McCullers novel, which he still had within reach.) "My dear enfant-terrible-poet-of-his-generation, shall we?"

"I've got nothing to add to the conversation I had last month with His Excellency, President of the Republic."

"You're my witness, Colonel. We've done everything we can to extract this Leninist vermin from his arthropodic darkness. Those beetles must have the flame of martyrdom in their blood. But for you, Denizan Richard, this final posturing will be refused. Doc Duvalier and I have already thought of everything. We're concocting some very nice *requiem aeternam dona eis*–style\* plans to counter any of you Mulatto troublemakers. Go on back to your place in Bourdon. Beware of moonlit nights. Don't leave the capital without special authorization from the police. Colonel Marcellus won't be very inclined to grant it."

"You can count on me for that, Excellency."

"In lawful societies," I said, "we'd call that house arrest. Such a constraint, in any free and civilized nation, would require a preliminary democratic judicial decision." (Some suicidal impulse was churning in my guts.)

With these words, Barbotog, literally mad with rage and looking every bit the tropical SS officer, got up and stood over my armchair.

"Lawful society! Democratic judicial decision! Free and civilized nation! Here's where you can baptize your white Occidental trinity: in the name of the Father, the Son, and the Holy Spirit!" he screamed, gripping his crotch and shaking it in his balled-up fist. "Only recently," he added, "that gazetteer Yvonne Kima-Rimini and her bitch daughters got a taste of this, like the Mulatto cunts from Pétionville they are. You've got a mother, sisters, cousins, and above all a gem of an Israelite wife. They'll get their turn with the wake-up-cockadoodledoo of the *papas-coqs-guédés*† of the Duvalierian revolution—all the way up their goddamn assholes!"

"Denizan's a lost cause, Excellency," said the colonel, affecting a false air of discouragement. "Let me take him back. I've got a few more things to add to keep him in order."

---

\* "Grant them eternal rest," first words, in Latin, of the Song of the Dead in Catholic liturgy.

† Vodou spirits, gods of death and copulation. They incarnate both Eros and Thanatos.

"That's fine, Colonel Marcellus. Get that worthless pile of flesh out of my sight. I get nauseous at the sight of any man who doesn't realize he's carrying around his own coffin!"

Accompanied by the colonel, I slowly retraced the hurried journey I'd embarked on with the lieutenant Fontoriol. Once we reached the stairs, the chief of police whispered in my ear:

"Please excuse me, Mr. Denizan. This isn't at all my way of doing things with a citizen of your stature. The talented surrealist poet Major Pol Morris-Leroy is my brother-in-law. He introduced me to your books. I liked them. You must understand, your days are numbered. Same goes for Madame Denizan. Your brother Régis and your Palestinian brother-in-law, notorious members of the opposition, are also on the list of future victims of Macoutist violence. Yesterday evening at the Palace, before the excursion to Bourdon, the militia's principal killers asked for the president's authorization to send the Denizans and Co. to kingdom come once and for all. Doctor Duvalier told them not to touch a hair on your heads for the moment. Nonetheless, he laid out his strategy for your family: 'We must take the time to come up with a death made-to-measure for that light-skinned Bourdon mob. I'm thinking up some special-edition disappearances. I'm honing sui generis methods of zombification for the whole Mulatto subspecies.' The Head of State and his gang are convinced that the Cominform has entrusted your interracial couple with the mission to prepare an insurrection of angry youth from the Haitian Left. The way the newspaper *Coumbite* welcomed you last December got them thinking. The invitation to dine at the Palace, the search through your library and requisitioning of your books, the contrived idea of a conspiracy with Picasso, Hemingway, Césaire, Breton, and McCullers—that's all part of Papa Doc's Mardi Gras. Pol agrees with me. There's only one way out of this situation for you and your family if you want to avoid the worst: ask for political asylum in one of the Latin American embassies."

"A thousand thank-yous. Coming from you and Pol, this advice is priceless."

At the exit, in the presence of the gatehouse officers, the colonel pretended to take his leave of me without the slightest graciousness.

"Citizen Denizan Richard, consider yourself warned. The next time, it'll be bang-bang-bang!" he said loudly and menacingly.

Over his shoulder, I caught a glimpse of the repressed scream behind First Lieutenant Leslie Fontoriol's eyes. For me, death had Lili's blue-green gaze.

# 7

# CRISIS CELL IN BOURDON

After the conversation at police headquarters, there was only one thing to do back home: gather together all the members of our endangered family in a crisis cell. Two people were missing at the dining room table: Lucie and Didier. Their membership in the Vodou National Salvation Front automatically excluded them from our council.

On hearing my account of what happened, Popa and my older sister Rita clasped their hands nervously over their mouths. From time to time, in reaction to something I told them, they emitted from between their teeth that sound that the solitude of misery extracts from the women of this island.

"Lord have mercy! Oh, my stars!"

"Miserere mei Deus!

Dito silenced her own terror. She was well acquainted with history's sharp turns. Many of her loved ones, Ashkenazi Jews, had disappeared in Chancellor Hitler's ovens and gas chambers.

As for the men of the family, Rachid, Guy-Luc, and Régis kept their heads in their hands, elbows propped on the edge of the table. My tale of meeting with the police confirmed the opinion they already had regarding the Vodou National Salvation Front.

"The VNSF," said Régis, "is the eraser that wipes out any trace of humanity in all men and women."

"They're concocting a collective zombification of the Haitian people," I said.

"We won't let ourselves be zombified," said Popa.

She had taken on the resolute air she reserved for tough times.

"Here we go," said Rachid. "Now von Hofmannsthal is *riding* Mama Popa."

Indeed, her gaze and her hands quivered as the white man from overseas began taking over her neurons. Her voice became harsh and determined. Her entire broken body became that of the Viennese theater prodigy that had *mounted* her.

"Dito has to get out of here right away. Her departure, heartbreaking for Dick, will be difficult for all of us," said the *lwa*. "Is she not another true Haitian living under my *horse's* roof? Nonetheless, it would be unjust to expose her, defenseless, to all the abominations here."

"I've seen plenty of those, you know," said Dito, throwing her arms around the shoulders of her *lwa* von Hofmannsthal of a mother-in-law.

"This is the second time," said Popa, "that my daughter-in-law has a bunch of SS-Macoutes on her heels. Too much, that's too much for one lifetime. You're an only daughter. Your parents need you in Tel Aviv. Dick will join you there, God willing."

"I agree," said Rachid. "With her Israeli passport Dito can leave without a problem. With my help, Dick and Régis will get asylum in a South American embassy: the Brazilian and Venezuelan ambassadors are my bridge partners at the Circle Club in Port-au-Prince. Mama Popa and Guy-Luc have nothing to fear. They weren't involved in any of the nonsense around the last election. As for Rita and me, we've already prepared everything necessary to leave for Miami with our boys."

"Rachid is right," I said. "Dispersing is the only option when you've got nothing but bare hands to face off against a despot. But as for me, there's no way I'm leaving."

"Have you gone mad?" said Guy-Luc.

"For the time being, I'm the least vulnerable of all of us. Papa Doc will need time to work out the made-to-measure death he's got planned for these bones of mine. He's set himself a challenge for this country: to turn us into a herd of zonbi. Well, it's a bet! I'm staying with the Haitian people to take him up on it."

"You're completely out of your mind," said Guy-Luc. "Your kamikaze move won't help anything. This idea of some kind of worker-peasant movement is nothing more than a bunch of soap bubbles. There's no way Comrade Kola's red army can administer the rules of good manners and revolutionary civility to a Nazi cyclone. What's keeping you here with us, in this bubble of black smoke?"

"We still might be able to forge a path," I said.

"The people of Haiti just need men of action to show them heretofore unheard-of ways to fight against barbarism," said Rachid.

"Dick and Rachid's ideas aren't unreasonable," said our mother. "By staying, Dick wants to show that one man, even all alone in a ditch with the other defeated, can still help his fellow citizens to rise up against the storm."

"Bravo!" cried Dito. "Mama Diani has just put forward an epidemic view of freedom, like there's nothing to it. This is the same idea we find in Jean-Paul Sartre's theater. It's called contagion by example."

"She's come up with some pretty turns of phrase our Popa-Sartre!" said Guy-Luc, "except for the fact that playing the solitary hero here in Port-au-Prince isn't a head cold you can pass on to your neighbor. One poet's solo battle can't do anything to open the eyes of the living dead."

"You've done enough talking, Guy-Luc," said Régis. "Let our mama *horse* finish up her Sartrean reasoning."

"What I'm saying is that, even before Papa Doc and his Nazi zonbi, the mortal enemy of this skinned beast of a Black republic is the idea this country has of a Haitian-style Republican State."

"From that has emerged our hatred for any sort of social contract, our longstanding disdain for the rights of man and the citizen, our mystical vision of all matters related to civil society," I said . . .

"Then," added my mother, "there are the cyclones, malaria, drought, infant mortality, the atrocious ordeals faced by every household; you have to add to that prostitution, erosion, yaws, malnutrition, floods, and all the rest; and on top of that, a whole pile of serious miseries to come—it's all part of the same Baron Samedi–style Black power that makes Haiti an existential hapax!"

"You mean to say that we experience our social iniquities and natural disasters as equally magical phenomena," I said, "as if State Tonton-Macoutism, Papadocracy ad vitam aeternam, homegrown and imported despotism, and carnivalesque politics all have the same supernatural origins as the winds and rains that devastate banana plantations?"

"Yes," said Dianira Fontoriol. "Papa Doc's totalitarian Negritude is the cosmic obscenity created by the sorcerers of barbarism."

"It's a Black power *vlanbindingue,*\* for Chrissakes!" Guy-Luc cried out, enraged.

"Does that mean we're forever doomed, here in this bloody shambles of a nation?" asked Régis.

"It's wrong to exaggerate our tribulations like that," said Rachid.

"True," I said. "Talking like that really isn't very clever."

"There's still a way to climb out of the ditch of SS-Macoutism," said Rachid.

"Faced with the pack of hyenas that is the National Front," said our mother, "there are still grounds for the Haitian people to brace themselves on their feet, their knees, their hands, their guts . . ."

". . . and on their big hooters, too?" asked the always dirty-minded Régis.

"Indeed, let's not forget about the beautiful solar dimensions of the body," said our mother.

---

\* Name of one of the black magic sects that have evolved on the fringes of the Vodou religion.

"Including the semiautomatic crankshaft of our macho-men and the dream-boxes of our local gals for good measure. If this country is going to be rebuilt, it'll need some lovemaking and childbirth like nothing we've ever seen before!"

With these radical words of hope, our first family council ended in good spirits.

# HAPPY ARE THE FEET OF
# THE MESSENGER


In that same issue 2, volume 1, the gazette of the rising
generation feted the return of a poet who was thought to be
gone forever, far from the travails and the days of desolation
in his homeland. A host of welcome pieces were dedicated to
him with the headline, "Hello, Richard Denizan! Hello, Dito
Sorel." Pages and pages of top-notch writing—in Haitian
and in French—rolled out a red carpet beneath the feet of
Dick Denizan, the non-prodigal son, really more of a trea-
sured son, because he has come back to the home of Dianira
Fontoriol, wrote Lucien Leprieur in his editorial. Well before
him, a wise man from the Far East once said that the ideal
is a matter of generation: it is why so many young people
in Dick's age group welcomed him with open arms upon
his arrival at the dock in Port-au-Prince and in the columns
of the local newspapers, after eleven years that were, in the
course of their old chum's life, like the eleven stations of a
nomadism that might be compared with the fate of the Indian banyan tree:
     at the doorstep of your country, dear brother, we say:
     praise be to your libertarian nomad's journey
     here you are, back under our roof in Bourdon
     on the left, the sun gathers
     the blue crowd of your dear friends
     your blood flows back into the Gosselin River, which car-
ries the news straight to the musical ear of the gulf of Jacmel.
In these scorching times, your return is the most refreshing
tree. This return-of-daybreak-coolness enchants the little
madan sara bird up in the hills; and also the Creole-speak
of our hot sauce and the vivacity of marine salt. This return

opens up the grammar that rules over the ABCs, within the alluvial order peculiar to the DNA of Grandma Celia, our childhood Grande-Ya, radiant in her nightly liturgy, whose military Vodou guided the airborne roots of your banyan tree

we slaughtered the fatted calf on your return; the table has been set beneath a flowering mango tree. Eat well of the warm, tender food, cooked in the fresh butter of friendship. Here are all the local dishes we have prepared for you: red beans and rice, flavored with djon-djon mushrooms and z'oiseaux peppers; the fish has been prepared in a sauce des dieux; the chicken has been grilled and soaked in enough juices to delight your taste buds. Let your mouth give in to the temptations of yams and ripe plantains; of guava and soursop juice; give in to the male tongue's craving for the sensual tropical papaya. In your state of exotic qui vive, give in to the great hunger for the corn that smiles from ear to ear, to a cousin's moist garden during summer vacation, supremely Haitian and ready to eat, to embrace, to ravish at daybreak, wonder of chocolate and cassava; or to the evening of adolescence, illuminated by Lili's royal fanny

with the same furor, open up the labyrinth of this incredible third of an island; without hesitation, approach General Alphénix Ultimo's musician trees, high up in the hills of Jacmel; blend your globe-trotting breath with the tragedy of crucified seasons; open up the Seven Sorrows of the rainbow that created you: purple Monday, indigo Tuesday, blue Wednesday, green Thursday, yellow Friday, orange Saturday! And now you have returned, on a quest for the red Sunday that rolled in the soil of the ancestors with the flabbergasted head of the great Generalissimo Phénix Ultimo on a ceramic plate

in his General Sun's finery, the celebrated writer Jean-Alex Aldébaran went down to the port to meet his companion: *Merry Christmas, Richard! Merry Christmas, Dito!* The morning has launched its rose-colored flares over the hills

in honor of your couple; joyous skies emerge alongside the
flame trees, blue, clear, upright, perhaps alongside a butter-
fly, a rogue petal, the volatile downiness of the humming-
bird; hitch yourself to this once-in-a-lifetime flight, to the
immense diamond of the Caribbean Sea that, in all the days
you've been journeying toward us, waiting for the sound
of "Land, ho!," has been carrying the soft, dense earth of
this uncertain December—this tenderly native earth—from
island to island. For both of you it is a Venusian call, endless
and of undefinable scent, to the garden of its blossoming
lasses; your mother will come as the magical Popa Singer,
as a medium, her eyes the color of the island seasons; your
mother, the one-and-only von Hofmannsthal, hands undone
by a sewing machine used to stitch up the ugly sheets that the
great history of humanity has made of our lives! There on the
dock of your return, your mother, in a state of possession,
along with your sisters and brothers and several friends, has
released the doves of an unprecedented act of welcome

do you remember, asked Jean-Alex, the cheap little hotel
on Joubert Street (3 Joubert Street, in Paris, right behind
the Galeries Lafayette department store), where we stayed
when we got to France? Paris was generous and trusting with
our adjoining rooms. Paris enhanced the wine of our young
lives. Paris helped us to study, to create, to live intelligently
in the miseries of those times. Paris delivered our senses to
the greater harmonies inspiring us to work, to laugh, to sing,
to ski, to swim, to read, to drink, to fuck recklessly, in the
hopes of one day making the tender notion of fraternity
flourish across the world

having been the first to welcome you to that foreign land, I
welcome you back to this twelfth nativity that, this time, you
will deliver from the soil of home, which is the very essence
of your manhood, and which gives us the zest for life—Hallelujah!—time will pass, arms will embrace you so that you
might better participate in the stirrings of life, in the human

despair of existence, in the mystery and solitude within each one of us—man, woman, and child. Now we are going to create, to get old, to enrich ourselves with passion. We will take on bitter struggles. We will have to roll up our sleeves if we are *to win the battle for the human heart.* To the honor and satisfaction of existing—let us sing, drink, rejoice in the rediscovered island. Merry Christmas Dick Merry Christmas Dito—in the radiance of the highlands of Haiti!

# THIRD MOVEMENT

# 8

# SONATINA FOR AN UNHAPPY
# LOVE STORY

On the evening of Dito Sorel's departure, after a final meal
with the family, Régis picked us up in his convertible jeep at
eight o'clock. The June sky was ash-dark. A rainy wind blew
through the oven of a gelatinous and desolate Port-au-Prince.
Whirlwinds of dust harassed the remaining passersby.

In the welcome office at the port, we sleepwalked through
filling out the final embarkation forms. The cargo ship *Carolina* would be leaving for northern Europe. Six months before, that same Dutch steamer had brought our family from
Rotterdam to Haiti. Now it seemed a bit worse for wear on
the deserted wharf. Régis feigned needing to fill up his tank,
a pretext for leaving us to say good-bye to one another without any witnesses.

Suddenly we found ourselves entangled in the bonds of our
marriage. Feverishly we grasped at one another's hands. The
preceding days, on the margins of the chaos swirling about
us, we had subjected the history of our relationship to an
exemplary housecleaning. We let absolutely nothing slide. We
admitted our mutual guilt: in the time of a general cold war,
we had both done our utmost to set fire to the little shack that
had served to shelter our years of conjugal drifting.

In these moments of separation, I made no effort to understand how the feeling of disenchantment felt for her. Within
me, it was a low-grade pressure. In another few unpleas-
ant minutes, the Dutch trading ship would steal from us the
packets of sunlight we had unabashedly created in room
301 of the International Student Housing Pavilion in Paris.
On that April night in 1950 my *little soldier* had celebrated
"the beginning of the world." With brushstrokes worthy of

Courbet, his unprecedentedly energetic state offered every ounce of my life force to the enormous appetite of a marvelous love-box.

"You are a lovebird from a Hebrew fairytale. By infusing my veins with the gluttonous paradise of your lust for life you have turned my days into sweetly Judeo-Hungarian bliss. Portico rose of Jerusalem, climbing rose on the wall of my jubilations, together we perfectly embody the angel-with-two-backs. Beneath the navel of your beauty, my wandering Jew of a paintbrush, unsheathed and searching, experienced one hundred years of a dazzling intimate carnival before disappearing one night into the flames of $x^n + y^n = z^n$ laying in wait, catlike, between your garden-woman's thighs!"

At the moment of our separation, in the very depths of my solitude, there appeared a vagrant who had no desire to retain in his shadowy realm that sumptuous force of Jewish electricity encountered at the Sorbonne. Our atoms were not destined to remain madly intertwined for life. My innate maleness, obsessed with the damp chapel of femininity, ended up transforming our passion into unbearable summer storms. I'll be damned if my poet's evening greeting hadn't lost both its cool and its heat while possessing the fanny of its dreams.

Well before the vessel's final maneuverings, the rain that until then had been a steady sprinkling of warm water suddenly began to beat down on the port. Its downpour mercilessly drowned the puppy dogs of our farewell embrace.

I watched Dito in the stormy onslaught as she made her way up the plank, more charmingly garden-woman than ever before. From the bridge, as she headed toward her cabin and into eternity, her wave good-bye was accompanied by a most sorrowful grimace.

An entire lifetime before, in an amphitheater at the Sorbonne at the conclusion of Gustave Cohen's course on lyric poetry of the Middle Ages, the same expression of woeful tenderness had preceded by just a few hours the sun-filled evening in a student bed at the Rosa Abreu de Grancher Foundation, better known as the Cuba Pavilion, at 59A Boulevard Jourdan.

Behind the wheel of his jeep, Régis came back to drag me out of my shipwrecked state. Without the splendor of Dito by my side, I had suddenly become a survivor of an unhappy love story in the whirlwind of humanity. I wouldn't stop singing at the top of my lungs a famous little tune from back then: *There's no such thing as a happy love story.* The June weather, like a cruel old uncle, struck my little brother and me violently from behind, driving us back to the little wood house in the heights of Bourdon.

# 9

# THE BEST MAN

"How cruel it is to be alive, oh Our Lady of Good Remedy!" whimpered my sister Lucie, her voice choked with sobs. "Our best man did this to us. How hard this is to bear!"

"Tell us what happened, dear Cici," said Dianira Fontoriol to her youngest daughter.

"Yesterday at noon, Didier and I were about to set the table when the phone rang. Clovis Barbotog informed us that he'd be making a stop at our place in the early evening, 'to talk about some business not unrelated to giving lessons in Greek,' is what he said. Completely flustered by the news, Didier thought our friend Totog planned to serve us—right on a silver platter—that position he'd been after for so many months: Haitian Ambassador in Athens. At exactly seven o'clock he showed up wearing his Tonton Macoute chief officer's uniform. He was flanked by Boss Gros-Bobo and L'il Râ Bordaille, his first deputies in the militia. Immediately after sitting down, he began showering Didier with foul language. 'Listen here, Master Jeannotin, you stale coconut-headed Greek professor,' he said, 'our Spiritual-Leader-for-Life nearly lost his mind when he found out that you continue—despite our clear guidelines—to spend your Sundays stuffing your face at your wife's family's place in Bourdon, in the company of our Mulatto enemies. We care for you too much at the VNSF to imagine there could be any betrayal on your part. At the same time, our political office is allergic to the Mulatto-Greco-Latin humanisms to which your professorial navel remains attached. You're going to have to cut the Gordian knot. Tonight we've come to bring you willy militari into the sanctuary of Negritude. The extra-territorial L'il

Râ, specialist of our offshore foragings, is harboring—right there in his pants—the right piston for revving up any waning of your ethno-Duvalierist calorie intake,' is what he, the distinguished sponsor of our honeymoon, said to Didier, oh Our Lady of Perpetual Remedy."

A crying fit even more intense than the previous one once again silenced Lucie.

"What happened afterward?" said Popa, panicked.

Undone by emotion, eyes drowning in sorrow and shame, Lucie became overcome by the anguished words flooding her from head to toe.

"Was Didier repudiated?" asked Popa.

"Is your husband in prison?" I asked.

Lucie shook her head violently in denial.

"Have mercy on me, Lord!" said Popa, making the sign of the cross, like me, having thought the very worst.

"No, don't worry, Didier is still alive. He's completely shaken and can't rise from his bed of disgrace. Totog did this to us, in public, at seven o'clock in the evening—Saint Antonio de Padua, have mercy on our star!"

"I'll bet," I said, "Professor Jeannotin was tied up, on his knees, arms behind his back, in a corner of your garden, to be whipped by L'il Râ."

"Worse than the blows of the rigoise,* Dick. Talk about a reverse caning! Virgin of the Bronze Charity! Pray for Didier's Ursa Minor!"

"My sweet fountain of mercy," implored Popa, "drink the dregs of your goblet of affliction. Enough tears. Tell your troubles to your loved ones, it'll do you good. Tell us!"

Lucie took a handkerchief out of her bag. Popa helped her to wipe her flushed cheeks.

"The sidekick L'il Râ," she stammered, "tied Didier up. He bent him over the dining room table. He smashed his face into the fruit basket. Then, oh my dears, oh! he pulled down his trousers and his underpants."

---

* Braided oxtail whip used for corporal punishment.

"Smack, smack! The old Greek received a homespun spanking!" said Popa.

"Talk about firing a retro-rocket! My classical culture husband had to quietly stomach more than twenty knots of tailwind!"

"Didier was *papadoc-ed,*" I said.

"Your Thermopylean husband has no more North Star to guide him," quipped Popa.

"Or Panama Canal either!" lamented Cici, having a hard time suppressing her urge to laugh.

"How did you react to that affront?" I asked.

"In fact, there was a double violation. Boss Gros-Bobo kept me at bay, an open razor to my throat, so that Clovis Barbotog could fiendishly feel up my Maginot Line. Under different hands (and along different pathways), Didier and I screamed simultaneously with the pleasure-disgust being extracted from our entrails. On leaving, the head Macoute arrived at our front gate and then turned and walked back up the driveway. He whispered in my ear: 'Congratulations, my dear goddaughter, there's a real woman under that dress of yours! As for Master Jeannotin, L'il Râ's methods must be quite familiar to him: wasn't that the goddamn favorite pastime of the gods of Olympus, which your numbskull of a professor imposed as a model for our high school students?'"

"In your place," said Popa, "I'd have given him a good slap!"

"I did better than that, Mama: I spit in his face," confessed Cici, before collapsing with fright.

# 10

## THE EVENTS OF JULY 29, 1958

What happened in Port-au-Prince at daybreak on July 29, 1958? It had been a month since Dito Sorel had returned to Israel. Following a brief period of asylum in the Brazilian embassy, filled with bitterness, with raging resentment in the pit of their stomach, it was Lucie and Didier's turn to flee the Haitian wasps' nest in mid-July. In those days, Rachid was traveling in Miami for business. His successful fabric business brought him there regularly. This time, Rita accompanied him, along with their children. The following Sunday, at the weekly lunch at Bourdon, there were no more young couples around Popa's table.

"Miserere mei Deus! my hearth has been whittled away! Watch out for yourselves my sons!"

At three o'clock in the morning we were awakened by the deafening sound of gunfire. Long after sunrise, all sorts of cracklings and bursts of machine gunfire had us holding our breath. The battle seemed to be taking place in the area surrounding the Palace and the streets of the Champs-de-Mars. We were at Bourdon, not three kilometers from the "theater of operations."

Seated at the table next to Popa as we sipped our stronger-than-usual morning coffee, Guy-Luc, Régis, and I got caught up in speculating about whatever was going on in town. We finally settled on what seemed like the most likely scenario. After months of quiet rivalry, Barbotog's militia was doing battle for real. It was pretty clear that the police would be the biggest losers in this settling of accounts. They no longer had access to their own stores of weapons and munitions. Ever since the Kima-Rimini affair at the end of February,

informed of the growing discontent of certain Mulatto officers, Papa Doc had the basement of his palace converted into
the sole arsenal of the Republic. He keeps the keys within
reach day and night. By holding firmly onto his adversaries'
weapons, he meant to cut off the provisions for any possible
coup d'état.

"If the police force has decided nonetheless to risk everything," said Régis, "their military leaders risk finding themselves pretty quickly down at Fort Dimanche, facing the
bullets of a firing squad. The Tonton Macoutes will leave
them no quarter."

Our mother folded in on herself, listening intently to our
uncertain early morning predictions. Rather than jump into
the conversation, she sat stone-faced for a long time. Her
eyes lowered on her mug of café au lait, she seemed to be preparing for the return of her spirit guide with renewed fervor.

"Von Hofmannsthal isn't on our same wavelength,"
teased Guy-Luc.

"You see, to my mind," she said, suddenly in the mood
for a fight, "Kébreau's gang has nothing to do with this
early morning skirmish. It's more likely an uprising among a
civil sector of the opposition. During our last family council
meeting, Rachid said some extraordinary things. But they
don't seem to have roused your imagination. Rachid said:
'Haitians just need men of action to show them heretofore
unheard-of ways to fight against barbarism.' He added:
'There's still a way to climb out of the ditch we've been dug
by the Tonton-SS.' At the end of the meal, he all but spilled
the beans entirely: 'Rita and I,' he said, 'we've made arrange-
ments to leave for Miami with our sons.' That bug didn't fall
on a deaf woman's ear."

"You're talking to us as if at this very moment you can
*see* Rachid stretched out behind a bed of hibiscus on the
Champ-de-Mars, firing a machine gun at our enemies!" said
Guy-Luc.

"Second sight has never been my strong suit," said Von
Hofmannsthal. "I'm only able to assist Dame Fontoriol,

*horse* of my dreams, as she gallops just a step ahead of the tragic events befalling this country. That's all I've got: your mother can stake her life on it. This very night, her son-in-law Rachid Ben Estefano, Palestinian husband of her daughter Rita, father of her two grandchildren, has thrown himself body and soul into the coup that's tracking that wild animal Papa Doc right to his lair!"

The news had us completely titillated, like each time our mother gave a sign of her marvelous gifts as a *lwa*-medium. But what my brothers and I later heard on the tyrant's radio broadcast about the story of what had happened the day before took our breath away. In this tragic beginning of September 2001, returning to this moment from the past, forty-three years after the tragedy of July 29, 1958, I find myself even more astounded.

"This past night, at around three a.m.," said the *Voice of the Haitian Republic* broadcaster, "after taking the Dessalines Barracks—adjacent, as everyone knows, to the main hall of the Presidential Palace—a commando arriving from Key West, Florida, came within an inch of capturing the Chief Spiritual Leader-for-Life of the Haitian Third World in his sleep, without a fight.

"Rest assured, dear listeners, that we are decidedly a very lucky people: as we speak, the valiant presidential troops have already disarmed the pack of white mercenaries brought to desecrate the home of Emperor Jean-Jacques Dessalines the Great by former Mulatto officers in collusion with the capital's Syrio-Palestinian merchants. At this very hour of the morning, their bodies have been left to the vengeance of fundamentalist ethno-Duvalierism. These vagabonds of the international underworld have been abandoned to the ultimate justice of the good Lord's flies, hanging below the president's balcony, which overlooks both the history of the world and the grassy esplanade of the palace.

"These pirates of the full moon were eight in number. The riddle of how they managed it has been solved at the headquarters of the Vodou National Salvation Front. With the help of the police, the NSV was very quickly able to identify and follow the thread of their machinations. After traversing the thousand or so miles separating the straits of Florida from our Gulf of Gonâve, they disembarked from the *Molly C,* a 55-foot motorboat.

"As to the Haitians on the crew, there were two Mulatto ex-captains: Sonson Pasquier and Angelo Albi, flanked by ex-first lieutenant Phil Dominguez, whose skin was even fairer than that of the other two. During the time of Colonel Paul Magloire's dictatorship, these officers straight out of a bad silent film—aces at scheming and porno shindigs—were the pillars of an unofficial organization known as Paulie's Little Junta. Their Haitian-style shadow cabinet was effectively the right hand—the oppressive, wheeler-dealer right hand—of the man with the iron shorts, who, back then, created more hurricanes than good weather in Port-au-Prince. With his fall in 1956, his protégés ended up following him into exile in New York.

"Two of the five white adventurers on the crew, Arthur Payne and Dany Jones, were deputy sheriffs in Dade County, not far from Key West. The other risk-it-alls were Robert F. Hickey, Levant Kersten, and Joe D. Walker, the captain of the *Molly C.* Covered in obscene tattoos, those carnival-wrestler physiques were surely recruited from the Miami underworld.

"Identifying Joe D. Walker has been no small feat for our able detectives. Indeed, although severely mutilated by the enraged crowd, the skipper's body is the spitting image of the Syrio-Palestinian merchant Rachid Ben Estefano. That morning, on the park benches of the Champs-de-Mars, the vox populi was letting it be known that if it wasn't Estefano himself, then it was certainly his white-American-*marasa*. The two hoodlums, the dead one and the living one on the lam, look so much alike they could be mistaken for one another. It took a thorough examination of the crew list for the investigators to sort out the unsettling confusion. Note, however, that this doesn't mean our Mister Ben Estefano has escaped the scene of the crime and the ensuing investigation.

Indeed, the *Molly C* was found tied to the dock of his cottage in Déluge, the locality of the disembarkation. As if by coincidence, the Levantine gentleman of Fronts-Forts Street is sojourning in Miami with his entire family these days. As the investigation continues, it will surely be revealed that, in addition to the infamy of having a Siamese twin brother at the helm of the pirate ship *Molly C,* Rachid Ben Estefano is the civilian silent partner of last night's desecration.

"So they cast anchor yesterday, July 28, in the early afternoon, in Déluge, a small, sheltered cove on the northern coast, right between Montrouis and Saint-Marc. The residents of the area, mainly fishermen, well used to yachts stopping over, paid no attention to all the commotion being made by a bunch of swimsuit-wearing white guys scattered around the beach. Taking them for tourists, the vendors rushed to sell them straw hats and carved wooden trinkets made by local artisans. By the same token, no one was surprised by how assuredly they brought the *Molly C* up alongside the landing pier of Rachid Ben Estefano's bungalow.

"In the course of the evening, the boat's captain easily got Saul Petit-Frère, a local tap-tap driver, to rent him his vehicle. The pretext he gave was needing to be in Port-au-Prince early the next morning to get a replacement for a defective part of his motor. He'd had some mechanical issues during the journey there. The assailants waited till nightfall to load Petit-Frère's tap-tap with trunks full of weapons and munitions. A notebook found on the ex-captain Albi revealed that the criminal operation had taken the baptismal code name 'Dry Clean First Thing in the Morning.'

"Dressed in the khaki uniform of the armed forces, the commando drove by the light of the full moon toward Port-au-Prince without raising the slightest suspicion among the military posts of the northern coast. At around three in the morning, the guard on duty at the Dessalines Barracks found himself facing a hot-headed Mulatto captain ordering him to open the heavy iron gate. His jeep had broken down on the road to Léogane, so he had commandeered a tap-tap for the transport of a handful of white prisoners dressed up as policemen. He had just subjected the drug traffickers to a muscular interrogation.

"Once they passed through the entrance to the barracks, Pasquier Sonson handcuffed and gagged the dumbfounded sentry. Then the tap-tap crossed the exercise field before stopping at the foot of the stairway leading to the guardroom. The three soldiers on duty—two officers and a sergeant—had their throats slit immediately, without even realizing what was happening to them. After the triple murder, the felonious Mulattos, thanks to their perfect familiarity with the place, unleashed the white brigands on the Black garrison. Our ebony brothers were jolted awake by the butts of guns and insults in English. In their undershirts and underpants, completely disoriented, they were bound with twine and locked up, like so many sacks that had been emptied of live coals.

"Having seized control of the Dessalines Barracks, the evildoers had less than a thousand feet of yard to cross in order to penetrate—O sacrilege!—the bedchambers of the presidential couple. But the guardian angels who watch over the sleep of their Spiritual Chief led the ex-captain Pasquier to waste a lot of time on the telephone. They robbed him of the element of surprise, which, up till that point, had assured the mission's success. Sonson Pasquier felt in his gut an urgent need to call some soldiers he knew, with the idea of recruiting them to his mission. One after the next, he got them on the line—the army and the police headquarters, the commander of the Coast Guard, the commander of the National Penitentiary, the director of the Military Academy, the president's godson, and even the ever-faithful Claudius Rémont, the very young captain who commands the Presidential Guard. Vacillating, in Creole, between words of triumph and vulgar swearing, he told his interlocutors that a thousand men with heavy artillery, having taken over the Dessalines Barracks, had just surrounded the National Palace and the principal buildings of Port-au-Prince. Thus was the government of 1957 overthrown: the ex-president

François Duvalier had twenty-two minutes to pack his bags. The Colombian embassy awaited him and the members of his immediate family.

"The events might well have taken the turn imagined by the megalomaniacal delirium of the ex-captain Pasquier. His forty-five minutes of blustering on the telephone was enough to sow confusion in the ranks of the police, at the office of the VNSV, in the government, and among the security forces. In the Vodou land of Haiti, that meant failing to account for the Spiritual-Leader-for-Life's closest alter ego: the enterprising Baron Samedi.

"Beyond the distraction he worked on Pasquier, he also had recourse to a strategy worthy of a true emir of a Muslim cemetery. The ex-captain Albi suddenly felt a kind of craving in his balls, almost libidinous, to smoke a Splendid cigarette in the morning light, with its earthy smell of a Haitian woman. Baron Samedi reminded Albi that the stalls at the Salomon Market, a hundred yards from the barracks, were open all night. Hard as a Polish buck in the Philadelphia Zoo, the ex-soldier immediately removed the handcuffs and gag of the guard Grégoire Titus-Pierrot. He ordered him to make like the wind and go buy him two packs of Splendid. Once his feet hit the pavement, our nationalist-Duvalierist Titus-Pierrot, godson of L'il Râ Bordaille, more profoundly Macoute than anyone else, headed straight to the Palace military post, sprinting like Zatopek himself. He told Captain Claudius Rémont that he had an ultra-confidential, personal message for the President from Baron Samedi. Papa Doc stopped preparing his panicked departure. He had the soldier sit down in his lap to uncover the mystery of his destiny.

"'Excellency,' said Titus-Pierrot, his teeth chattering, 'Baron Samedi wants you to know that the invaders are no more than eight brigands: three pitiful Mulattos and five white Americans with more tattoos than a Croix-des-Bouquets tap-tap!'

"Papa Doc asked Titus-Pierrot to repeat what he said twenty-two times in a row: he didn't have a thousand men

with heavy artillery to reckon with, but only the lousy bluff
of some filthy little Mulatto ex-captain!

"'Yes, Ritual-Father-in-Chief,' said Titus-Pierrot, dazzled
at the conclusion of his early morning litany, 'nothing but
eight hairless pigs decked out in the khaki uniform of evil.'

"The Spiritual-Leader-for-Life immediately had a few bot-
tles of champagne opened: he had to drink immediately to
Baron Samedi and to his L'il Pierrot messenger. The political
*lwa* of our Haiti are stronger than the Palestino-Mulatto
merchants and the police force gathered around a pentacle
of sheriffs!

"Still in his black silk pajamas, the President went back
to his bedroom to change. In the hallway, he was practically
shimmying as he walked away: he indulged in a few rabor-
daille dance steps that had the members of his inner circle
laughing through their tears. He reappeared a few moments
later: dancing this time in full combat gear, a metal helmet
on his head, two Colt 45s on his waist, brandishing a Belgian
assault weapon and a brand new Fal rifle. He cut short the
cheers and congratulations of his courtesans.

"'Quiet, comrades, for fuck's sake! My bacoulou-baka
balls are hungry. At noon, I want someone to bring a bowl
of formaldehyde—that's $CH_2O$ goddamn it!—with the head
of that preening piece of trash Pasquier Sonson to this table!
I want the balls of that dumbass, Splendid-chain-smoking
fanatic in a bowl of whipped cane syrup! A curse on their
grandmother's clitorises!'

"Dear listeners, this war cry, shouted from the heights
of ethno-Duvalierist fundamentalism, did not rally merely
the hyper-machos of the NSV, police officers, sailors, avia-
tors, firemen, and members of the Vodou National Salvation Front. Swept into the early morning on a thunderous
wave of *télédyòl,* the Spiritual Chief's call ultimately brought
together an unprecedented politico-military carnival: patty
vendors; milk sellers; vegetable producers; surrealist hooker-
hetaerae, still in their most incendiary form; obscenely
empty-bellied shoeshine boys; insomniac yard boys; sassy

beggar-children-of-the-national-sidewalks; drivers with tattooed skin like the sides of taxis and tap-taps; Neo-Thomistic philosopher-vagrants; early morning Negritude wanderers; an entire Haitian universe of enraged folks gathered as a single block around their President and his Macoute militia. The Palace Guard hurriedly distributed rifles, bazookas, grenades, and even a few torpedoes (requisite insularity!) for the relentless assault on the desecrators of the Duvalierist revolution.

"Dear listeners, in this radiant hour of victory over the troublemakers, come see them on the lawn of the National Palace, caught in the sybaritic jurisdictional grip of the mistress-flies of Baron Samedi! Rififo Fonthus-Figaro's well-placed grenade artfully decapitated the ex-captain Pasquier. There he is, ready for the President's jar! The ex-lieutenant Phil Dominguez seems to be cozily napping on his daybed, despite having caught a Springfield shot in the right ear, some exemplary punishment in each eye, not to mention the bullet that Commander Barbotog's Sten machine gun misplaced in his enormous dick, well seasoned by the orgies of garrison life. Come see the ex-captain Albi, evermore asleep in the lecherous smoke of the native land; he was treated to a last pack of Splendids: the warm hands of a young milkmaid from Croix-des-Missions piously placed it on the gaping hole he earned for himself right in the upper back.

"The white mercenaries, transformed into five old sieves, also aren't too nice to look at under the ferocious sun of the enraged Haitians gathered on the square. The highlight of this spontaneous Mardi Gras was undoubtedly the corpse of Joe D. Walker, enigmatic captain of the *Molly C.* In the crowd's effervescence, everyone heard about his suspicious resemblance to the Palestinian merchant from Fronts-Forts Street. A few sentimental individuals wanted to hold on to an intimate souvenir from the countryside by dipping the corner of a handkerchief in the porridge of gray matter strewn across the lawn. The mystical volcano of hatred, the inferno of curses and expletives in Creole, immediately found some release in a devilish merengue melody. Its refrain took to task, in a single torrent of reprobation, Mulatto treachery, the piracy of sheriffs, the barbarism of Rachid Ben Estafano's murderous Islamism. At this very moment, the song, which definitely has it in for Paulie's Little Junta, continues unabated to contribute to the general jubilation of an entire race on the Champ-de-Mars. On this historico-cultural morning, the illustrious Tonton Macoute François Duvalier, more the adoptive son of the Holy Scriptures than ever before, has emerged the omnilateral victor of the first trial by fire of his mandate as President-for-Life!"

Following that radiophonic victory report, my brothers and I stayed silent for what seemed like an eternity, our eyes—shining with despair—turned toward our mother. Not one of the three of us dared speak a word before the woman who had seen these events coming.

"I didn't get it wrong," she said. "Last June, the night of our crisis cell meeting, Rachid tried unsuccessfully to inform you all. What he said was the precursor of the armed action he was plotting with his buddies in Florida."

"To lose it all that close to the goal—what a bunch of inept screw-ups!" said Régis.

"What bungling weaklings!" cried Guy-Luc.

"That successful coup gone in a puff of cigarette smoke, it defies all understanding!" I said.

"For me," said our mother, "the men they massacred are neither tinkerers, nor jokers, nor sons-of-bitches. And they weren't bewitched by the SS-Tonton-Macoute cesspool either. In their stupid debacle, they remain heroes nonetheless. My *horse* will confirm it. She has a high opinion of the three former police officers. In the forties, Popa hung out with their relatives in Bois-Verna. Later, during the time of Paulie's Little Junta, they helped her make ends meet from time to time, without ever requesting any in-kind services from my *horse*, although your mother was a mare who could have held her own with any stallion!"

"They were real bambocheurs," said Régis. "I ran into them at the masked balls in Pétionville. Disguised as the three musketeers, they were throwing holy oil galore on the flames of their partners, dressed up like sultanas from *A Thousand and One Nights!*"

"On that front, it's true," said our mother. "That three-some had a gift for partying. They loved beautiful, warm flesh—the passion for life of a great Creole orchestra! All the same, the *télédyòl* never said anything about them pillaging the State till or torturing people in the basement of the Des-salines Barracks. Their little junta would have slightly lim-ited the damage of the elite satrapy reigning in the shadow of General Paulie Magloire!"

"Do you think Rachid thinks as highly of them?" I asked.

"My *horse*'s Arab son-in-law wouldn't have called on their qualities as men of action if he thought they were piti-less bastards without law or *lwa!*"

"Can we say as much for their white companions who went down right along with them?" asked Guy-Luc.

"In my eyes," said von Hofmannsthal, "those Yankees are no gangsters. At worst, a bunch of thrill seekers who were looking for a high-stakes weekend in a 'magic island' off the coast of Florida. Maybe—and why not?—those boys had some American notions of democracy to instill in their neighbors to the south."

"Rachid must have let his checkbook do the talking . . . ," said Régis.

"Of course," said the *lwa*. "They wouldn't have risked their lives for Rachid's Palestinian jade-green eyes alone. Even so, their human substance is the direct opposite of Papa Doc's 'Black' filth."

"Skin color has nothing to do with what happened," I said. "In his National Palace here in Port-au-Prince, barbarity is 'Black.' Right across the way, in the Dessalines Barracks, a doomed patrol of 'Mulattos' and 'whites' defended—per-haps absurdly—the beautiful light of humanity!"

"The fact remains," said Guy-Luc, "it's the Black people leading the carnival of barbarians in this country!"

"Yes, Guy-Luc," said the *lwa,* "the good guys sometimes help the bad guys crush other good guys. And so miserere mei deus! as my *horse* would say, war among humans is never a question of good guys and bad guys, saints or not. A tiny lamp of peace, still just a babe, has long sought to bring us all closer to the human condition. On the other hand, the infancy of a rogue lamp works to distance us from our panhuman identity. That's perhaps the best-kept secret in history . . ."

"The eternal guerilla war between immature little lamps has yet another new eternity before it!" said Régis.

"In the meantime," said Guy-Luc, "here we are in a fine mess. The reprisals won't be long in coming. We won't count for much in the Macoute mousetrap. By Saint Peter's balls, the barbarians are here!" Guy-Luc exclaimed in a panic, at the sound of screeching brakes punctuated by gunshots in front of the house.

Our mother rushed to the door. She returned, alight with a refreshing burst of laughter.

"A few Tontons and some police officers—completely naked, shouldering assault rifles—stopped and shot into the air, very pleased to make a U-turn in mid-route. They greeted me with another volley of shots before disappearing in the opposite direction. They're all caught up in their drunken victory celebration!"

"Operation *requiem aeternam dona eis* against us has nonetheless begun. Over two months of harvest, it's taken not only Dido, but Lucie and Didier, Rachid, Rita, and our nephews."

"They're lucky to live far away from all our zomberies," said Régis.

"Whose turn will it be next time?" asked Guy-Luc.

"The vice is tightening around Régis and Dick. As for you, Guy-Luc, marriage, the bees, the royal jelly, the propolis—it's a good cover. Get out of this mess, nice and easy."

"Our mother," said Guy-Luc, "keeps hitting the nail on the head. I was just about to extend an invitation to you all: on September 22, I'm marrying Marie-Françoise Périgard. As of the 23rd, we'll leave to fulfill the contract I signed with one of my North American beekeeper friends who owns a farm in California!"

# 11

# THE NEVER-ENDING NIGHTMARE

Early in the morning, on July 30, 1958, Papa Doc donned the uniform he had christened the night before. He asked Fonthus-Figaro to draw up a list of those in the Military Academy cohorts—classes of 1941 and 1942—that Pasquier, Albi, and Dominguez had belonged to.

"It's no coincidence," he said, "that Pasquier tried to re-cruit classmates from his class that were stationed in far-flung garrisons in the backcountry. Esprit de corps is a powerful Mulatto trait among our police force. We're talking about truly unnatural beasts. Goddammit we're going to have to execute 22 of them at Fort Dimanche!"

"Clovis's wiretapping system recorded the calls from Pas-quier's rebellion," said Fonthus-Figaro. "He started off by reaching out to commanders at the Port-au-Prince central square. Then he communicated with thirteen military district chiefs in the provinces. He called nineteen superior officers. Leaving your dear godson Captain Claudius out of it, as he's beyond all suspicion, we've got a batch of eighteen suspects to put down."

"The list is missing four guilty parties. Ever since my vic-tory on September 22, my navel is forever linked to that fateful number. It's the crown jewel in my star. I woke up on this day with the following brilliant idea: the firing squad for the execution of Pasquier's 22 accomplices should consist of the 22 highest-ranking officers of the police force. The joint staff of the armed forces will receive the order to fire their Springfield rifles by some low-level soldier. Fifo, can you think of any better way to teach any of our potential enemies a lesson?"

"After the execution," said Fonthus-Figaro, "your Haitians will cry: 'Long live *papa-22-of-the-Republic-for-life!*'"

Things moved quickly. On the night of the 30th, the President convened his military chiefs Barbotog, Gros-Bobo, L'il Râ Bordaille in his office. Besides his faithful Fifo, his godson Captain Claudius Rémont and his secretary-concubine Francesca de Saint-Totor were also by his side. He informed them of his decision to liquidate, according to a sui generis ritual, the officers Pasquier had called instead of going straight for an assault on the Palace . . .

"It's proof," he said, "that far from suspecting them, he was confident they'd participate in the plan. Totor has typed up a list of the eighteen insurgents. We're getting close to the 22 of my propitious moon. Name four last-minute guilty souls of your choice. That shouldn't pose too much of a problem for any of you."

"There's one name that comes to me off the top of my head. Just last Thursday, Excellency, I heard you bitterly complaining about an officer in the Presidential Guard."

"I know the bastard you're talking about, dear Totor. In effect, my friends, for some time now one of my closest guardsmen has been appearing in my dreams in the form of a Saudi Arabian emir. With a machete in each hand, he demands the keys to my treasure: 'Your harem or your life!' he screams each time. I have finally recognized Captain Tédéhomme Maxisextus's voice. Aide-de-camp to the First Lady, this officer has been taking advantage of his proximity to my inner circle to play around, up close and personal, with the innocent sex appeal of our two little girls. That garrison playboy has indulged in some heavy fondling at the expense of my adolescent daughters' sacred fire. And it gets worse: even our chubby, plump little Jean-Jean—that future little devil of ours—hasn't been spared his wandering fingers. Lately his misconduct has gone up a notch in its scandal and profanation: after Carla, Maria-Antonia, Jean-Jean, and Francesca, Mama Simone, the Queen Mother herself, was subjected to her own bodyguard's goddamn gallant fingering! We can expect the worst: an attack on the decency of the Spiritual Leader isn't far behind. In trying to get off, with a few Te Deums here, a few laudamus-sextus there, Captain Maxi has placed himself phallically outside the law! And thus do we have our nineteenth convict for my list!"

"In the troop placed under my command," added Captain Rémont, "Maxi isn't the only one to have betrayed my godfather's trust. Late one evening last April 5, while I was taking a relaxing stroll in the park, I came upon one of the Monastir twins, Lieutenant Thomas, down on all fours in the grass with Carla, dressed in a baby doll nightie, straddling his back. I was about to react when the other Monastir brother, Lieutenant Wilfried, appeared with Maria-Antonia, in the exact same libertine position. 'What the blazes are you two lieutenants up to?' I cried. 'Just a bit of moonlight frolicking, Captain!' those indecent *marasas* and their consenting victims answered in chorus, without even interrupting their little game of double-dutch!"

"That's called killing two birds with one Springfield!" said the President dryly. "All we need is one more felon to pick up. A little effort now, comrades!"

"The lieutenant of the Guard, Jérôme Hilarius," said Boss Gros-Bobo, "has been exiled from the ranks of the Duvalierists. Last March, Mr. President, your famous speech to the students at the Ethnological College revealed to the country the three principal architects of the Haitian universe: the Deity, Dessalines, Duvalier. On that day, you made the three truly capital Ds of the Vodou pantheon shine in the eyes of our youth. On the day after the event, as I was celebrating that brilliant discovery with Lieutenant Jérôme, he spit out, disgruntledly, the following blasphemy: 'Three great architects of the universe, you say, chief—at the next carnival some grotesque carnival band is likely to turn the President's three D's into three fat *Derrières*-in-the-field!'"

"That's no surprise coming from him," added Barbotog. "The supreme D cherished by Lieutenant Hilarius is the papa-*lwa-Dollar*. Although he wasn't a part of our intelligence service, our twenty-second corpse was always holed up with that CIA operative in Port-au-Prince, Colonel Jimmy Dickenridge."

"Thank you all for your loyalty," said the President. "I'm putting Fifo in charge of inviting the 22 general staff members of the police force to be present at Fort Dimanche in black tie on the evening of August 5. Not a word to anyone about what I have in store for these gentlemen from the heart of the platoon."

On the morning of August 5, Barbotog informed the President that the twenty-two condemned men had been locked up tight for the past three days—"incommunicado, trust me, Mr. President!"—in Fort Dimanche.

"Bravo, dear Totog! Now that the Duvalierian iron is hot, we'll have to strike this very night, as planned."

Late in the evening, a convoy of official vehicles hurriedly took off from the Champs-de-Mars headquarters toward the northern exit out of Port-au-Prince. In Fort Dimanche, Tonton Macoutes armed to the teeth awaited the high-ranking military officers. Stationed up front, Barbotog played master of the house, shaking hands with the terrified men. He had a friendly and reassuring word for each soldier.

"A thousand thanks for coming. The President shouldn't be much longer. His Excellency intends to raise this August night to goddamn historically Elizabethan heights!" he announced to the company at large.

The soldiers exchanged the most forced smiles of their lives: how were they supposed to follow the head of the Macoute military in the mountaineering expedition he had in mind for that August evening? They waited for two hours (burning through more than one pack of cigarettes between their sweaty fingers) before Papa Doc arrived, wearing his

commander's uniform as chief of the NSV. He responded
to his twenty-two subordinates' solemn salute with a disgusted gesture of the index finger. He indicated for them
to follow him to the firing range, about a hundred yards
behind the prison's dilapidated buildings. At one of the far
ends of a floodlit clearing, the twenty-two condemned men
were already tied up, petrified with fright, each to his own
stake.

"Gentlemen of the national police," said the President,
"you all know I'm not one to beat around the bush. Therefore, without further explanation, I command that you 22
zonbi form the squad of executioners called on to ice the 22
traitors lined up here before you. Gentlemen commanders, I
said, form the goddamn squad!"

Like so many disciplined soldiers, trained either at the
school of the American *Marines* or at West Point, the officers
immediately formed a perfect line, facing their dumbfounded
and despairing buddies. L'il Râ Bordaille gave each of them
a loaded Springfield.

"Gentlemen, officers, before carrying out the orders of
your Supreme Leader, I invite you to listen to the words of
our distinguished ethnologist. Tonight, so as to do away
with this pack of traitors without any court-martial, I'm
disregarding the old traditions of the armed forces of this
planet. Each great democratic culture is free to cover its ass
however it wants, in accordance with the originality of its
historical roots. Why should my Haitians be the only ones
not allowed to cover the big *bounda* of their own cultural
identity? Tonight, I'm leaving aside any foreign models of
capital punishment. It'll be an ad hominem cap-in-the-ass
death sentence, Haitian-style, of course! In my death ceremony, the discharge of Springfield rifles will no longer be
unique, anonymous, or blind. I'm opting for shot-by-shot,
one after the next, fired on my orders, by a platoon officer.
In this way, each of the commanders of my police force
will have the luxury of looking into the eyes of the former
comrade in arms—the absolute bastard he's been called on

to hurl beneath the earth of the disrespected fatherland. This is the *Duvalierian* way of saving the honor of a police force that Pasquier, Albi, Dominguez, Ben Estefano, Arthur Payne, Joe D. Walker, Dany Jones, and other international mercenary sheriffs nearly dishonored for all time. With my zombification plan now in place, all that's left is the execution."

"Ex-lieutenant colonel Altidor Kesner, where are you, you monkey's miscarriage?"

"Here, Your Excellency," sighed the condemned man.

"Right, I see you. You've betrayed your benefactor out of loyalty to the class of 1941 Mulatto officers Angelo Albi and Sonson Pasquier. Your cousin, Colonel Officer Helder Wilfort, is charged with ending your lawless vagabond's maneuverings. Ex-lieutenant Altidor Kesner, for goddamn-fuck's sake—now fire!"

"Ex-lieutenant Nicolos Pépé, son of a harlot and big old whore yourself, where are you!"

"Here, Mr. President!"

"Right, I see your Mulatto whorishness, your buddy from the class of 1942, Major Ernest Chicognard is heating up—just look at him—with the idea of lighting up your bastard traitor's lungs with his Springfield. Goddamn-fucking ex-major Nicolos Pépé—now fire!"

"Ex-captain Te Deum Maxisextus laudamus! Where's your Latin canto of nimble acts of grace? Don-Juan-Casanova-*rara-band*-Marquis-de-Sade, where are you? Ah, ah, ah! You're sniveling in your disgraced officer's shorts! You aren't answering your President's call like a courageous macho-man? I send you back to the Mardi Gras of my nightmares like an Arabian emir with a screwed-up hard-on! For the last time I'm casting my eyes on the stalker of the warm bodies of State power, stalker of Papa Caesar's harem! Down with your lubricious crocodile tears! Down with your whore of a grandmother's clitoris! Your own brother-in-law, the sweet, surrealist Lieutenant Colonel Chris-Paul Lafalaize will snuff out, on my orders, your too-goddamn geometrically unstable libido from my household. Goddamn-fucking ex-captain Te Deum Maxisextus laudamus—now fire!"

The ritual was repeated twenty-two times in a row. The only minor setback was Captain Tédéhomme Maxisextus's crying fit. The other executions, notably that of the Monastir *marasa,* went like the bleakest clockwork.

# 12

# CLANDESTINE TRANSMITTER

My brother Régis heard the story of the Fort Dimanche executions from an eyewitness, a nurse friend of his who worked in the prison dispensary. On the same occasion, Régis revealed to Popa and me that a clandestine transmitting station, Radio Liberty, of which he was the director, would soon be divulging the episode he had just recounted to the public. The scoop of the inaugural broadcast was planned for August 22, 1958.

Weeks before the "Sheriffs of the Full Moon Affair," Régis had decided to make an about-face from opponent to conspirator. Instead of a twinkling solar erotic being, he was, I discovered, a cold libertine, hearty and hale, who had accepted all the risks of clandestine combat. Without us noticing, he had rapidly become the primary liaison for the opposition leader Marc-Antoine Grandet. Head of a handful of courageous supporters, the latter was fearlessly organizing, from his hiding place, a network of resistance to the State's terrorism.

Besides Régis Dénizan, Radio Liberty's other right-hand man was a merchant of Cuban origin who'd lived in Port-au-Prince for many years. Tonio Alvarez's launderette—*El Oso Blanco* was its name—was situated on the northern side of the Champ-de-Mars, at an equal distance from the Palace and the headquarters of the police and the armed forces. It was separated from the President's office by two hundred yards of lawn, as the crow flies. It was truly the one place in town where Barbotog's henchmen would be least likely to look for the radio waves emitting anti-Duvalierist propaganda.

To move around safely, Régis sold the old roofless jeep that he was known for in the neighborhood. He bought a little used Morris, discreetly adapted to his conspiratorial activities. To von Hofmannsthal's great joy, he was proving to be a master of disguise. He had been operating right under the nose of the Tonton-SS, disguised as a police officer, chef, itinerant monk, agronomist engineer, telegraph operator, stewardess, nurse, mailman, fireman, even a Sister of Charity. But whatever the chosen disguise, he was always the same person, wracked with the same despairing and humble fury. Whether engineer or mailman, he was consumed by the same rage and the same shame in the face of all the misery befalling us.

He barely lived in Bourdon anymore. He showed up at the house out of the blue every now and then. Knowing he was being tightly surveilled, he came and went by a path known only to us: at the back of the garden, down below, next to an unfrequented empty lot, traversed by a ravine that the rainstorms turned into a torrent of mud. On each visit, Régis showed Popa and me a different disguise.

On the afternoon of August 23, the costumed visitor who told us about the bloodbath at Fort Dimanche was wearing the white cassock of the Fathers of the Oblates of Marie. He had an enormous rustic wooden cross hanging on his chest. He had no other personal information to share with us. His humanity kept its head lowered, as much in the face of the great massacres of the world as in the face of the miniscule bits of popular disturbance he had just executed over the course of a long, torrid day in La Saline, in Bel-Air, in Bolosse, in Lakou-Bréa, in Tête-Bœuf, and in other neighborhoods of Port-au-Prince where hope has always hung on by an old bit of thread.

I did my best to help Régis's Radio Freedom broadcasts give Haitians the sense that they had come to an existential standstill inside a tunnel, out of which their third of an island risked emerging in a body bag. I wrote up the story of the executions he'd told us about in person. Tuning in to Radio Freedom took on an extraordinary importance. Only one thing mattered to the authorities: locating the source, at whatever the cost, of that hour of truth telling that, each and every night, exposed the Medusa's head of the Vodou National Salvation Front.

In vain, Barbotog oriented his hunt toward the residential neighborhoods of Pétionville, Croix-des-Bouquets, in the heights of Kenscoff and Furcy, and in the seaside communities of Jacmel. After several days of useless commotion caused by the Tonton Macoutes, the President decided to solicit technical support from the naval forces of the American army base in Guantanamo, on the western tip of Cuba. A US destroyer, on patrol in Haitian waters, received the order to disembark a team of tracking experts on the island. After a week of reconnaissance, they delivered a formal report to Duvalier: Radio Freedom was transmitting definitively from somewhere on the northern wing of the Presidential Palace.

The Duvalier family's private rooms were located in that part of the building. The famous *houngan* of Mirebalais, Victor-Hugo Novembre, resided in an employee's studio there, in his role as "special chaplain to the President of the Republic." Leaving his bedroom, Papa Doc had only to take a few steps across the Persian rugs to indulge in his secret consultations with Baron Samedi or with any other of the political *lwa* of the cemeteries Novembre had the power to summon.

Immediately after the US Navy experts' report had been translated into Creole, Papa Doc rushed to his official sorcerer. Victor-Hugo Novembre was not caught unawares by the revelation. His investigatory methods were just about to lead him to the same conclusion as the white American experts of Guantanamo with all their specialized knowledge. For several nights in a row, Baron Samedi, helped by the famous detective-god Ogou-Badaviolet, had noticed suspicious radio waves in the residential areas of the Palace. Whenever the transmissions stopped, the vagabond waves went roaming under Carla or Maria-Antonia's perfumed sheets.

"Once night falls, your mortal enemy," continued Novembre, "the defeated candidate from the last elections, that

pain in the butt Marc-Antoine Grandet, has the diabolical
ability to change himself into a clandestine broadcaster, from
whatever hole he's lying in wait in. He can transmit freely out
of your powder room or your toilet. If we let him, Grandet
will take on other forms of existence in order to destroy you:
shark-toothed grand piano in your Japanese sitting room;
black Labrador foaming at the mouth with pleasure right
alongside the epic orgasms of the presidential couple; an-
thrax epidemic mounting an attack on the blood cells of the
Vodou National Salvation Front. Transformed into a purebred dildo, he can perch the First Lady and Carla and Maria-
Antonia on his erect back like Amazons on some infernal
ride before subjecting them to the most first-class rollicking
in universal orgiastic history. Assisted by his brothers, all
of them militants of the hairless-pigs sect, he has metamor-
phosed into a Hertzian evening *télédyòl*. He has mounted a
campaign against your revolution. The entire Grandet family
must find themselves immediately in the formaldehyde jars
where we preserve the cutoff heads of our enemies. This is
the only way to silence Radio Liberty."

Papa Doc immediately agreed to the death sentence
handed down by Victor-Hugo. On the very night of the judg-
ment, he launched an island-wide manhunt for Grandet and
company. He gave the order to go through Port-au-Prince
and its surrounding area with a fine-toothed comb, house
by house, until all the Grandet brothers' hideouts had been
found. The directive was to slaughter the men and women of
the family, without sparing the children, relatives, and allies.
The hunt was to extend to all men and all animals who bore
the same first names as the Grandets: all the Marc-Antoines,
Ducasses, Charleses, and Clément-Napoléons were to be
eliminated. Also deemed outlaws were black dogs, of which
many wandered the streets; same went for grand pianos;
same went for live coals, often bringers of similarly named
political ills. So that the roundup would be successful, L'il Râ
Bordaille added owners of bars and brothels, bank employ-
ees, Jehovah's witnesses, bicycle repairers, and metalworkers

in the slums of the capital to the wide-ranging categories of civilians mobilized at dawn on July 29.

This new murderous carnival had everyone all riled up. Savagely terse watchwords were borrowed from legendary slaughters of the past: off with their heads and their balls! Screw their grandmothers and their godmothers all the way up their fat asses! Burn down their houses and the deeds to their property!

The settling of scores that the "depraved spawn of the Radio Liberty brothers" were aiming for spread rapidly to other sectors of the opposition. Victor-Hugo Novembre had all animals and even objects he deemed suspicious included in the repressive measures: black-feathered birds, horses with black coats, school blackboards. At the chapel of the establishment of the Sisters of Wisdom, a militiaman leader, having detected a certain family resemblance between the doctor Clément-Napoléon Grandet and the statue of Saint Mark the Evangelist, screamed at a group of uniformed Macoutes to reduce "that Grandet buried within the Apostolic Roman faith to dust."

On the church square, Boss Gros-Bobo grouped 22 women from 122 opposition families into five columns, each one bearing a 22-pound candle in her arms. He made them parade naked as a rapturous crowd hurled obscenities at them. It was the occasion for him to announce over a loudspeaker that the four Grandet brothers were killed while fleeing from a Port-au-Prince convent disguised as nuns.

The Grandet funerals put an end to the interminable week of burials. On the passing of the funeral cortege, the sovereign tenderness of the sumptuous August afternoon seemed to be the opposite of the desperately terrified convoy that followed the four hearses.

At the chancel of the church, the Grandets were lined up one next to the other under a single bed of flowers. At the foot of the altar, a dozen priests, both Haitian and foreign, served as deacons to the official bishops.

After twenty-five minutes of canticles and Latin prayers, screams of horror began drowning out the great organs, brutally interrupting the ceremony's heartbreaking musical pageantry. A hundred or so militiamen, shirtless, with red scarves tied around their heads, entered by the main entrance of the temple as well as from its side entrances, clearing a path to the catafalques with blows of their machetes.

In less than a minute, the coffins were abducted and whisked away. The nuns who tried to stop the quadruple kidnapping of the bodies immediately had their own lives reduced to purée. The rumor that had been circulating for the past week became the cruel reality of Saturday, August 29, 1958.

Papa Doc and his master of sorcery had lined up four sparkling new jars on a shelf in the basement of the Palace, ready to welcome the hearts of Marc-Antoine Grandet and his brothers.

"After the theft of their lives, their deaths have been stolen from us, too, along with our words of good-bye at their graves," the man disguised as an Oblate of Marie said to us, concluding his tale.

He had come to say good-bye to us before taking refuge in a South American embassy under his real name, Régis Denizan.

# EPILOGUE

Once admitted to the Venezuelan embassy following the bloodbath and the kidnapping at the end of August 1958, Régis quickly obtained safe passage to leave Haiti. Guy-Luc, in turn, was also quick to depart. On September 25, in the evening, a ceremony at the Church of Saint-Pierre in Pétion-ville sealed his union with Marie-Françoise Périgard, without much fanfare. Only a few close friends were present at the reception given by the bride's parents at their home on Boyer Place. The very next day, Pan American flight 642 brought the couple to California. (Decades later, our brother happily grew old on a farm near Salinas, at the head of a prosperous colony of bees, surrounded by grandchildren and great-grandchildren, the tribe of my grand-nephews and -nieces in the United States.)

The Sunday of Guy-Luc's departure, as soon as we had returned from the airport, my mother and I sat alone in the garden to think over the current situation.

"That's it," I said. "Papa Doc has managed to clear out your little house. I'm the only one left in the firing line of that assassin. My made-to-measure death will take him some time."

"Here we are," said my mother, "the last three combatants, counting von Hofmannsthal!"

"What can a trio of unarmed resistance fighters do in the face of such terror?"

"Dear Dick," said my mother, "ask the question directly to the mythical guest in my head."

That was the first time that I was going to sit down for a tête-à-tête with a *mother–battle horse,* without any witnesses, in her state of possession.

Dianira Fontoriol settled comfortably into the rocking chair. The convulsion that precedes the ritual trance traversed her entire body as her eyelids blinked rapidly. Her limbs, arms and legs, trembled. A total void took over her body, as if she was about to lose consciousness. Through a veritable doubling of her personality, the play of her physiognomy, her ragged breathing, the tone of her voice, and her gestures all sought to reflect the character of a white male. Hugo von Hofmannsthal appeared before my eyes with all the clarity one might expect from an elite spirit of his caliber.

"Von Hofmannsthal," I said point-blank, "your *horse* and I, would we now be completely defenseless in the face of this barbarity?"

"Dick Denizan," said the white *lwa,* "your struggle against the barbarians began as soon as you listened to that Radio Rebelde news bulletin that broadcasted every night from the foothills of the Sierra Maestra."

"Does listening to the voices of the guerilla forces of the Castro brothers count as resisting Papadocracy?"

"Yes," said my mother's spiritual guide. "You spoke fervently to my *horse* about a guerilla commando with an Argentinian nickname."

"Che Guevara," I said. "I heard a tribute to him that took my breath away. This thirty-year-old doctor radiates with such utopian generosity that, fighting alongside him, his fellow combatants can hear the gurgling that his fertile dreams make in his angry young man's head! I'm burning with desire to join those Cuban guerillas in the mountains."

"It's the right decision that we—my *horse* and I—want to see you make without waiting any longer. From the locality of Cap-à-Fou, on the northwest Haitian coast, to Chivirico, on the Cuban coast, it's just a quick three-hour journey by sailboat via the Windward Passage. Fishermen dot the area each night. For next to nothing, one of them will drop you somewhere in Cuba. It's time to stop drying your poet's laundry on the clothesline of Haitian-style Stalinism. Once on

Cuban soil, join up, heart and soul, with the M26-7* of the
Castro Ruz brothers.

"Joining M26-7," I said, "will allow me to kill two birds
with one stone: escape from a 'made-to-measure death' and
from the terrorism of the Haitian Stalinists."

"With a little luck," said the *lwa,* "you'll be one more
Cuban in the Castrofidelist revolution."

"And what will I do," I asked, "if Cuba, in turn, strays
from the ideals of the October Revolution?"

"In the French elsewhere of Haiti," said the *lwa,* "you'll
be prepared to stand strong, always on alert, as you've
learned from my *horse.* Her feminine musicality will be a
force of illumination in your journey, comparable to that of
a princess of the ancient Orient once risen in the offended
memory of her time to foil the base maneuvers of humanity's
animal nature!"

"Popa Singer-Hugo von Hofmannsthal," I said, "might
this be the double authority that has been called on to fertil-
ize the Indian summer of my writings?"

"My *horse* and I," said the *lwa,* "we invite you to take
from Haiti the very incandescence of its endless tragedy so as
to blow the glass of the poet's tender word."

* The July 26 movement, created in 1953 by Fidel Castro following
the fall of the commando assault he had led on the Moncada Barracks
in Santiago de Cuba.

# INSTRUCTION MANUAL

At the root of the state of possession of Dianira Fontoriol, alias Popa Singer von Hofmannsthal, emblematic figure of this book, there is the purchase she made of a Singer sewing machine in a store in Jacmel. The German shopkeeper, to escape from the police in his country, had put out a sign on his seaside establishment with the name of the famous Austrian author Hugo von Hofmannsthal. Such are the constitutive circumstances of the *lwa*'s rhizomatic identity, which, in this story, is incarnated in the life of a Haitian mother.

I originally sent the manuscript to a publisher without including an instruction manual. Very awkwardly, I had submitted for his astute reading a story in which, bizarrely, one sees a mechanical object made by white people, a master of poetry and of Viennese theater, mounting—like some *lwa-counselor*—the head of a *horse* who was helping her family resist during an era of barbarity.

The story, written in the tradition of the Haitian marvelous real, without any keys for reading it, was unpublishable. It spent years in the darkness of a drawer. As a result, this failure rendered me incapable of finishing a single one of the fiction projects among the outstanding synopses on my worktable. My narrative silence was absolute, without my having been stricken by the syndrome of Bartleby, Herman Melville's famous character. My crisis of novelistic writing, even in its most acute phase, did not keep me from writing poems and short prose essays.

Today, the reader has before their eyes a composite of the Haitian imaginary code: human beings, animals, objects, vegetation; as well as natural phenomena (rivers, seas, cyclones, volcanoes, earthquakes); and supernatural phenomena (*lwas,* states of possession, epiphanies of Vodou gods) form a cosmic whole out of the adventure of common human being.

www.ingramcontent.com/pod-product-compliance
Lightning Source LLC
Chambersburg PA
CBHW030907050726
47500CB00009B/1152